A Whole New
Ball Game

by Belle Payton

Simon Spotlight

New York   London   Toronto   Sydney   New Delhi

This book is a work of fiction. Any references to historical events, real people, or real places are used fictitiously. Other names, characters, places, and events are the product of the author's imagination, and any resemblance to actual events or places or persons, living or dead, is entirely coincidental.

SIMON SPOTLIGHT
An imprint of Simon & Schuster Children's Publishing Division
1230 Avenue of the Americas, New York, New York 10020
Text by Sarah Albee
For information about special discounts for bulk purchases, please contact Simon & Schuster Special Sales at 1-866-506-1949 or business@simonandschuster.com.
Manufactured in the United States of America 0414 FFG
First Edition 10 9 8 7 6 5 4 3 2 1
ISBN 978-1-4814-0641-3 (pbk)
ISBN 978-1-4814-0642-0 (hc)
ISBN 978-1-4814-0643-7 (eBook)
Library of Congress Catalog Card Number 2013946996

CHAPTER ONE

"It's soooo hot in Texas!"

"It's soooo hot in Texas!"

Alex and Ava Sackett blurted out the same words at the same time. They did this a lot. Their mom always said it was a twin thing.

"If someone handed me a pair of scissors right now, I'd chop off my entire ponytail," said Ava.

"Then I suppose it's a good thing the scissors are still packed in a box somewhere," sighed their mother.

Alex rolled her eyes. "Must you always speak in such hyperbole, Ava?" She bumped her sister over a fraction of an inch. "Don't hog the fan. And don't even kid about chopping off your perfect, gorgeous curls!"

The two girls were sitting on the floor, sprawled against the wall of their new living room, sharing a single, not-very-large fan.

"Who's kidding?" Ava replied, bumping her sister back. "*You* have perfect, gorgeous curls. My hair is just a giant pain."

"What are you talking about?" Alex asked indignantly. "We have the exact same hair!"

As she spoke, Alex patted her own hair as if to make sure it was still there. It was, of course—piled into a topknot that was both stylish and practical in the scorching heat. Ava's chocolate-brown curls, on the other hand, were gathered into a messy ponytail. Loose strands had escaped and were plastered to her neck, making her even hotter. Ava couldn't help but notice that Alex's hair had stayed put on top of her head and wasn't stuck to her neck.

"Girls, it's too hot to bicker," said Mrs. Sackett. She'd given up trying to unpack the kitchen and was splayed in the one chair not stacked with boxes and other junk. She lifted the already-melting, ice-filled bag from the top of her head and applied it to the sides of her neck, like she was dabbing herself with perfume. "I'm sure your father will have the AC up and running any minute now."

From the office, Alex and Ava's older brother, Tommy, let loose a triumphant cry. He appeared in the doorway holding a second fan above his head, like a wide receiver who'd just scored the winning touchdown. "Found it!" he said, shoving a box out of the way to plug it in. He, too, slumped to the floor to bask in the flowing air, which rippled his own brown curls.

Ava got tired of jockeying for space in front of the fan. She stood up and drifted lazily over to the window, which looked out over the backyard. Beyond the fence was the backyard of the house on the next block in their development, and beyond that, a vast, treeless landscape, flat as an ocean, all browns, grays, and gray-greens. The colors in Texas were very different from the lush darker greens of their backyard outside of Boston.

Across the room she could see through the doorway into the kitchen, where their Australian shepherd, Moxy, lay on her side, panting. The kitchen floor was probably the coolest surface in the house, but that wasn't saying much. Moxy looked at Ava, the whites of her eyes visible as she gazed upward, as if asking Ava to explain what on earth had happened to the Sackett family. One day they were in Massachusetts, with a backyard full of squirrels to chase and lavish garden beds to dig up, and the next they were in dry, barren Texas, where it was too hot for any self-respecting dog to even *consider* chasing after a squirrel.

Ava cinched the elastic tighter on her brown ponytail. Long hair was bad enough—it must be awful for poor Moxy, who was basically wearing a fur coat right now.

Suddenly there was a groan and a whir and then a *whoosh*, and the air conditioner started up. All four of them cheered. Almost immediately, cool air began flowing through the house.

"Thank goodness," said their mom.

"Here comes Daddy," said Alex, as they heard footsteps bounding through the kitchen.

Coach Mike Sackett stepped over Moxy and joined his family in the living room. The air-conditioner repairman followed behind him.

"Much appreciated, Bill," said their father to the repairman, shaking his hand.

Bill saluted. "No problem, Coach," he said. "I'm sure y'all will get used to the Texas heat eventually. Must be quite a change from where you folks came from."

Coach nodded. "We'll get used to it, and everything else," he said, leading the man toward the front door.

"Practice start tomorrow?" Bill asked.

"Yes sir, it sure does."

"Team look okay?"

Coach chuckled. "We're young. It's going to be a rebuilding year, but I have high hopes for the boys," he said.

Ava watched her father, who was standing with his back to her, gently urge Bill toward the front door. At over six fot two, he towered over the repairman.

Bill hovered in the doorway, not yet ready to leave. "So what's your strategy against Culver City, Coach? I was talking to some of the guys at the shop, and they were saying Culver's got more size this year. You'll probably want to spread the field, right?"

Coach patted him on the back and guided him out the front door. "That makes sense. I appreciate the perspective," he said, and waved the man out.

"Another football fan!" said Mrs. Sackett with

a little laugh as Coach shut the door. "There seem to be a lot of them in Ashland!"

Coach grinned. "It's just the culture," he said. "Lots of die-hard football types. It was the same way when I was growing up around here. Everyone in Ashland pays attention to the Ashland Tigers. It's a nice, close-knit community, Laur. You'll see."

The cooler air flow seemed to have loosened Alex's speech.

"Okay, so, Mom," she said, reaching for her phone and opening her digital notebook. "We were discussing my bedroom. I've narrowed down my options under each of the following categories: curtains, bedspread, throw pillows, accent pieces, and paint colors."

Ava half listened as her sister chattered. Alex was thrilled about decorating her new room. Ava, in contrast, hadn't given much thought to hers. She wasn't sure she even liked having her own bedroom. She'd had trouble sleeping the whole four nights they'd been in Texas.

"What color do you want for your room, Ave?" asked her mother, who was peering into a box she'd just opened marked LIVING ROOM STUFF. She grimaced and closed the box again. "I still can't get over the color the last people chose to paint it."

"Mustard yellow," said Alex, wrinkling her nose.

"Yeah, we should probably paint over that," said Ava with a laugh. "You can paint it something neutral, I guess, so it won't clash with my sports posters. Beige is fine."

Alex looked at her sister in mock exasperation. "Beige is most definitely *not* fine, Ave! Not when you have the opportunity to pick any color you want!" When her sister shrugged, Alex turned to their mom. "Mom. Are you positive one of us wasn't switched at birth? How is it possible that Ava and I are sisters?"

"You two *are* so very different," admitted their mom. "But I can't help noticing that there is a strong sibling resemblance."

"Well, *I'm* going to go reassess my color choices," said Alex, jumping to her feet. "Even if *some* people couldn't care less what color their room is. I found this cool new home decor app called ColorSchemer. It has a built-in color wheel that lets you explore different shades and hues and combinations."

Ava felt a pang of hurt. She wished Alex

weren't quite so enthusiastic about the fact that they had their own rooms. To be honest, Ava had missed having her sister with her during this first week in their new house. For twelve years, their entire lives, they'd shared a room. She missed their old room back in Massachusetts, where they'd moved their two beds into an L shape, the better to whisper to each other late into the night.

In their old bedroom, Alex's side had been painted in retro colors. She had a neat book-case, and her bed was always tidily made. On the wall above her bed, Alex had created a col-lage of carefully arranged pictures of movie stars, the latest fashions, and some of her favor-ite quotes from people like Eleanor Roosevelt and Maya Angelou.

On Ava's side of the old room, the bed had never been neatly made—what was wrong with just flinging the coverlet up over the pillow? Clothing had a tendency to trail out of dresser drawers. Stray socks found their way under the bed. And *her* wall had been adorned with sports posters. Her half of the baby blanket they shared—their mom had divided it when they'd both wanted the same blanket back when they were little—lay in a rumpled heap under the covers. Alex hid her half every morning, neatly folded in her side-table drawer, in case someone should show up in their bedroom unannounced and tease her about it.

Well, their separate rooms were just one more new thing to add to the list of stuff Ava would have to get used to, along with this new house, new school, new neighborhood, new town, new state . . . new life. There were moments when she felt as bewildered as Moxy.

"I'm going to watch some film," announced Coach.

"Ooh! What film are you going to watch, Daddy? Can I watch with you?" asked Alex, who had paused in the doorway.

Now it was Ava's turn to look at her sister in exasperation.

Coach grinned at Alex. "Not *a* film, honey. Just '*film*.' In this case, footage of last year's squad, so I can get a better sense of the strengths and weaknesses of our returners."

Alex pouted. "Oh, right. Never mind." She headed upstairs.

"Tommy, maybe you want to have another look at the playbook?" suggested their dad.

Tommy sighed and got wearily to his feet. Ava still wasn't used to her brother's newly acquired height, or the fact that he seemed to get wider every time she looked at him. Sixteen-year-old boys were scary creatures. Everything seemed to happen so *suddenly*.

Alone with her mother in the room, Ava moved over to the window again and stared moodily outside.

Mrs. Sackett softly cleared her throat. "Anything wrong, pumpkin?"

Ava shrugged. "Nah. It's just . . . different here. I'll get used to it. I guess I miss my old room. And—my friends and stuff."

"Have you heard from Charlie?" asked her mother gently, not probing.

Ava nodded and swallowed. "Yeah. I think we're good. I guess he's really excited about football this year—he's been practicing a lot."

Charlie was her best friend back in Massachusetts. Alex was better friends with Charlie's twin, Isabel. Ava and Charlie had been inseparable since T-ball days. Their moms had met at a group for mothers of twins when all the kids were babies, and they had remained good friends. But in the past year, things had been . . . different between her and Charlie. He'd suddenly blushed practically every time she said anything to him. Pass the ketchup, please. Blush. Want to have a catch? Blush. That kind of thing. Well, maybe it was his red hair. Redheaded people blushed easily.

With a heavy sigh, her mom picked up a box marked KITCHEN STUFF. "It's hard for all of us, Ave," she said.

Ava looked at her in surprise. She'd been so busy wallowing in her own self-pity, she hadn't thought about this being hard on her mom. *But, Ava reflected, it must be.* Her mom had been really happy back where they used to live. She'd taught art at the local elementary school. She'd had her own friends. A garden.

"Dad is under a lot of pressure as the new coach, and Tommy as a player, too." Ava's mom broke into her thoughts. "At least you and your sister have each other. That's a really special thing."

Ava grimaced. She missed her sister, too. She missed the way they used to hang out together, to take Moxy for walks together, to wash up at the side-by-side sinks in their old bathroom every night. Now they tended to go to bed at different times, and the new bathroom only had one sink. Alex was monopolizing it; she spent what seemed like hours in there with the door closed, experimenting with different hairstyles. Just this morning she'd informed Ava that topknots were the Next Big Thing in hair trends.

"It seems like we're more different than ever. She's so 'go, go, go!' right now."

"Honey, that's just your sister's way of dealing with all these changes," Mrs. Sackett said. "I know she's been a little . . . intense lately, but she'll be calmer once we've all settled in. You know she feels better when she's working on some sort of project—picking up in Texas where she left off in Boston is her new project."

Ava thought about this. Her mom was right—Alex didn't like change. When she was five, she had thrown a fit when their mom started buying a different brand of peanut butter.

"But you know she needs you to pull her nose out of her planner once in a while," Mrs. Sackett joked.

Later that evening, after another takeout dinner sitting on top of still-packed boxes, Ava stood at her windowsill, listening to the night outside. In spite of the newly functioning air conditioner, she'd opened her window a little so she could hear the sounds of her new backyard. Back in Massachusetts, she'd loved to listen to the crickets and tree frogs. Here, everything sounded strange. She heard the steady, high-pitched drone of insects. A bird was calling *wooo! whuh-whuh-woooo!* over and over, and something large bumped against her window. Was it a huge moth? A bat?

"What are you doing, Ave?"

Ava jumped and turned to see her sister in the doorway, in her pajamas with a toothbrush hanging out of her mouth.

"Are there bats in Texas?" Ava asked.

"Yup, lots," said Alex. "Why?"

"Just wondering," said Ava. "You going to bed, Al?"

"Yeah," said Alex. "I just came to say good night. Wow, it feels weird to have to come say good night to you." She hesitated for a moment, bouncing back and forth on the balls of her feet.

"It is weird," said Ava.

Ava thought about telling Alex she missed sharing a room with her, but before she could put the right words together, Alex turned and went to spit out her toothpaste in the bathroom.

"Well, see you tomorrow!" she called as she went into her room, stepping over Moxy in the hallway.

Poor Moxy was so confused. She'd always slept in the girls' room, in the area between their beds. Now she didn't know what to do. The night after they moved in, their mom had found Moxy lying in the hallway between Alex's and Ava's rooms. Mrs. Sackett had dragged the doggie bed out there for her.

Ava climbed into her own bed. She was just drifting off to sleep when her phone vibrated.

It was Charlie.

Hey, what up? All good in Texas?
You wearing cowboy boots and
a ten-gallon hat yet?

Ha. As if. I'm just trying
not to roast to death.
It was over 100 degrees
again today. ☹

Whoa. You need to find a pool.

Yeah, I think there's one
pretty close to here. We haven't
had time to look for it, though.
How's practice going?

Doesn't start for three weeks.
We're not on the crazy
Texan schedule, remember?
Ha ha.

Oh right. Ha ha.

Ha ha. Well, CU L8ter.

CU L8ter.

Ava read and reread Charlie's texts. Her first-ever potential crush now lived 1,983 miles away. And her twin sister was sleeping a whole room away. Sigh. Both felt worlds apart.

CHAPTER TWO

The following afternoon, Alex sat at her new desk. She bit her bottom lip and frowned at her computer screen. Should she do aqua as the accent color for her new purple color scheme? It was amazing how many details one needed to consider when designing a room. Every choice was perplexing. Or was "agonizing" the better word? Yes, every choice felt agonizing. She couldn't wait until her room was all set up—then she could relax a little.

Ava had teased her for years about her excellent organizational skills, like they were a bad thing. What was wrong with choosing your outfit and laying it on a chair the night before school? Or ironing your T-shirts before you put them away? Or coordinating the color of your cardigan with the color of your headband? She smiled, thinking of how different she and Ava were when it came to getting ready in the mornings. It was usually a mad scramble to find Ava's other shoe, or her math book, and once or twice her sister had actually missed the bus. When they were younger Alex used to say she was more responsible because she was twelve minutes older.

Alex turned to the neatly stacked pile of pictures on her new desk. There were lots of shots of her and Ava. They'd dressed identically when they were little—their choice—and had delighted in being confused with each other, even, from time to time, by Tommy and their dad. Their mom never mixed them up—it must have been a mom thing.

She found a picture of her and Ava taken a couple of months ago, at the sixth-grade end-of-year party. Their outfits were totally different, because they had stopped dressing alike by then, but with their matching grins and identical long brown curls, they still looked exactly alike. Alex smiled and put the picture in the "yes" pile for her new oversized bulletin board. She loved pictures that showed how identical she and her sister were on the outside. Alex knew they were different in a lot of ways, but she preferred to focus on their similarities. And besides, even if she was a little disorganized and didn't care enough about important things like color coordination, Ava was still the best sister in the world. Alex felt lucky she had a twin, a best friend, to move across the country with. She vowed to try to help Ava fit in, be more organized, and make friends at their new school. These things just came more easily to Alex.

Alex was trying to decide which picture of her and her friend Isabel she should put up when she sensed her sister in the doorway and turned. She and Ava always seemed able to feel the other's presence.

"Studying your flash cards?" asked Ava with a grin.

"No, I did my five words already today," said Alex.

"Oh, well, that's a relief," teased Ava.

"It gets a little boring to learn them alphabetically, so I got daring and shuffled them up," she said with a smile. "Today I learned 'perplexing,' 'stupendous,' and 'agonizing.' I already knew what they meant, of course, but I'm also trying to practice using my vocab words in everyday conversations."

"Al, you realize you are the only middle schooler on the planet who is already preparing for her SATs," said Ava.

"I know," said Alex with a sunny smile.

"Seriously, how is it possible that you love school so much when I would stop going right now if I could?" Ava asked.

"How is it possible that you love football so much when I would never go to a game if Daddy weren't the coach?" countered Alex.

"Fair point," Ava said cheerfully. "Anyway, are you ready to go to dinner?"

"Where are we going?"

"There's a barbecue place across town. One of Coach's assistants told him about it. Evidently half the town eats there. The other half eats at the place across the street."

Alex grinned. "Stupendous. Maybe we'll meet some of our new classmates. I'd better rethink my outfit."

Ava rolled her eyes. "You look fine to me. But whatever. Mom says be down in five." She turned to leave.

"Hey, Ave?"

"Yep?"

"Um, Ave?"

"Still here."

"Do you think you could call me 'Alex,' not 'Al,' when we're around other kids? 'Alexandra' would be fine too. 'Al' just doesn't sound very sophisticated."

"I never call you 'Alexandra,'" said Ava. "But okay, I'll try not to call you 'Al.'"

"Thanks," said Alex. "And maybe you could call Daddy 'my dad' rather than 'Coach' in front of other kids too."

"That I won't do," said Ava. "I've called him 'Coach' our whole lives; it comes naturally."

"I just don't want people here to think it's weird!" protested Alex.

Ava smiled. Alex noticed for the zillionth time how her sister's whole face lit up when she smiled.

"Too bad! There's no way our family is ever going to seem totally normal," said Ava in a sing-song voice, and she clomped down the stairs in her bright green canvas high-tops.

Alex sighed and checked herself in the mirror once more. Maybe Ava was right about the outfit. She didn't want to look like she was trying too hard. Her periwinkle T-shirt with the scalloped hem did look pretty nice. Periwinkle was one of her favorite colors to wear because it went so well with her dark-brown hair, green eyes, and pale skin. She was wearing it with a white skirt that stopped a few inches above her knees. She wondered if she should put her hair up. Even though it was after six, it was still baking hot outside . . . but she *was* having a great hair day. As a compromise, she slipped a hair tie onto her wrist.

She stepped over to her laptop and closed the open windows before shutting it down. In addition to her home-decorating apps, she'd also been researching last year's student government at Ashland Middle School, studying the names and faces of the kids. She wanted to be sure to recognize them if she ran into them. It was all part of her campaign to be elected to the student government. Who knew? Maybe she could pull off class president! She'd been the sixth-grade class president last year, and she had been counting on being seventh-grade class president this year. She was really hoping the move to Texas didn't have to ruin her plans.

"Alex! Come on, I'm starving!" she heard Tommy's newly deep voice bellow from downstairs. "Your hair looks fine! My stomach is starting to digest itself!"

Alex giggled and hurried downstairs.

The restaurant was called Jimmy's Pit Bar-B-Q. Alex wrinkled her nose as they entered the place. It seemed every restaurant they'd been to in Ashland so far smelled of smoky, bacon-y, meaty cooking. It wasn't a very welcome smell for someone who'd recently decided to become a vegetarian. But Mrs. Sackett had checked out the menu online and had assured her that they had meatless options.

There was a line of people waiting to be seated, but when her father gave the hostess their name, they were ushered right in. Alex and Ava exchanged a look.

After they were seated, Alex scanned the menu with a weary sigh—ribs, brisket, sausage, pork loin, beef, *double* beef, whatever that was—and clapped it shut. "Looks like another scintillating night of cornbread, greens, and black-eyed peas for me," she said glumly.

Her dad looked at her over the top of his huge menu, his eyes twinkling. "Probably the healthiest things on the menu," he said with a chuckle.

Tommy nudged her with his elbow. "You picked a great moment to become a vegetarian. Who ever heard of a vegetarian from Texas?"

"All right, Tommy," said their mother. "Look, Al. There's a kid's menu on the back. You can get macaroni and cheese."

Alex flipped to the back to look. "Or a grilled cheese sandwich."

"Or a grilled cheese sandwich," said Ava at the same time.

The girls grinned at each other.

"Will you two stop with your weird twin thing?" Tommy asked them good-naturedly. "You'd think that—" He stopped.

A middle-aged man had suddenly appeared, standing close to their table, waiting politely for them to notice him. He was tall and burly with an impressive handlebar mustache. He wore a Texans hat and an Ashland Football T-shirt.

Coach got to his feet and shook hands with the man. "Mike Sackett," he said. "How do you do?"

The man pulled off his hat and nodded at the rest of the family. "Howdy, folks. I'm sure sorry to interrupt your dinner, but I just wanted to introduce myself and meet the new coach. I'm Floyd Whittaker. Mighty pleased to make your acquaintance."

The rest of the family smiled and nodded at him.

"I played for Ashland back in '79 when we won state. The year we scored with thirty seconds left and were down one? I was the running back. You probably heard about me? Coach decided to go for two, and I ran it in to win it all."

"Ah, yes. Thanks for introducing yourself, Floyd," said their father.

"I'll let you get back to your dinner," said Floyd. "But Coach, we're sure excited to see what your plans are for our boys this season. How's the team look?"

"Well, we're young," admitted their father. "And our defensive line could use a little more size."

"I hear you like to throw the ball. Not the way we've done it in the past," said Mr. Whittaker. "Always had excellent running backs here in Ashland, if you don't mind my saying so."

Coach smiled at him. "I'll talk about our options with my assistant coaches, and—"

Alex was relieved to see a young waitress approach their table to take their order. Mr. Whittaker seemed to get the message. He said good-bye and went back to his table.

Alex and Ava exchanged another look. Alex could see that even Ava, who loved to talk football, was unnerved by the intensity of Mr. Whittaker's interest in their dad's team.

The waitress took their order. Alex looked at Tommy with amazement as he ordered ribs and a side of sausage.

"How can you eat that much when it's so hot out?" Alex asked him, after the waitress had left.

Tommy raised one eyebrow at her. "I'm trying to put on muscle weight," he said. "I need my protein."

"Hello, Coach!"

"Howdy, Coach Sackett!"

A group of people—it looked like an extended family: young parents and their baby, grandparents, aunts, and uncles—passed their table and greeted the Sacketts.

Alex and her family all smiled and waved at them.

"How does everyone know who we are?" asked Alex.

Her mom patted her hand. "We're new in town," she said. "People are very friendly here. And they all love football. Tomorrow's the start of preseason, and everyone is curious about the new coach."

"So what are your plans for tomorrow, girls?" asked their dad, moving the conversation away from football. Alex always appreciated it when he did this.

"I'm going to start looking into trying out for the middle-school football team," Ava announced.

Alex gave her twin a pained look. What if Ava ran into a lot of obstacles trying to play football as a girl? It wasn't that big of a deal in Boston, but Texas was different from Massachusetts. What if it *was* a really big deal here?

"What? You don't think I should try out?" asked Ava, who had noticed Alex's look. "I was the best kicker on the Pee Wee team last year and—"

"She didn't say anything," Tommy pointed out.

"Yeah, but she *thought* it," said Ava.

"You guys need to stop reading each other's minds," said Tommy in exasperation.

"Enough," said Mrs. Sackett.

"Anyway, I thought I'd come to practice with

you tomorrow," said Ava excitedly. "I think some of the middle-school coaches might be hanging around, or at least that's what Tommy said."

Alex felt a pang of jealousy. She knew it was slightly irrational. Ava was her twin. Tommy was their brother. But she couldn't help secretly thinking that Tommy and Ava shared a special bond. They were both such good athletes. They'd clearly inherited the Sackett genes. Not the Wright genes, which Alex had obviously acquired from their very unathletic mother. At least she also had her mom's artistic sensibility.

Their dad smiled. "Okay, sport," he said. "That okay with you, Tom?"

"Do I have a choice?" asked Tommy, but he had a twinkle in his eye.

"How about you, darlin'?" their father said, turning to their mother. "What's your plan for tomorrow?"

"Well!" she said, her eyes shining. "I hear there's an excellent studio in town with a kiln. I'm thinking of resurrecting my pottery business, since I won't be teaching for the first time in a long time." Mrs. Sackett was waiting until the family settled in before looking for a teaching job in Texas.

"Mom, that's a fabulous idea!" said Alex excitedly. "I'll help you design a website!"

"Maybe we should wait till she creates some pottery to sell first," Ava pointed out.

"Alex likes to plan ahead, don't you, Al?" said Tommy. "Hey, how's your plan to take over the world coming along, anyway?"

Alex pouted. "I'm not planning to take over the *world*. Just the school."

Her dad raised an eyebrow.

Ava explained. "She wants to run for student government. But we all know her final goal is to be elected class president."

"So what if it is? It's been known to happen," said Alex. "I'm going about it systematically. I've looked up the rules on the school website. And I'm outlining a strategy to gain exposure right from day one."

"I'm sure you are," said Tommy. "Have you designed an algorithm for that?"

Alex was sick of Tommy's teasing. "Honestly, Tommy. Just because you're worried about not being the star quarterback anymore the way you were at Randall Prep doesn't mean—"

"Hey! Hey, now," interrupted Coach. "Let's not start—"

"Did I *say* I was worried?" Tommy shot back.

"What's *wrong* with me wanting to play football?" Ava blurted out.

"Kids! Please! Voices *down!*" said their mom, looking embarrassed.

Alex heard someone politely clear his throat. She looked up. Two men and a woman were standing next to their table, waiting for them to stop squabbling.

All the Sacketts froze and plastered smiles to their faces.

The people looked a little amused. Alex could feel her ears burning. Her family was fighting in public! That was *not* a good first impression!

Her dad stood up to shake hands.

"Just stopped by to meet the new coach!" said the lady.

The two men swept off their hats. "Welcome to Ashland, Coach!" said one of them, pumping Coach's hand hard.

Alex smiled weakly and slumped down in her seat. "Welcome to Ashland," she whispered quietly.

CHAPTER THREE

The following morning Ava settled into the bleacher seats at the football field and checked the huge stadium clock. Six a.m. sharp. It looked like all the players were on the field. *Nice to see these boys have discipline,* she thought. *And respect for their new coach.*

The sun had not quite risen in the eastern sky, but the morning light was golden, and the players cast long shadows across the turf field—an unnatural green color in this brownish-gray Texan landscape.

The team was assembled in six straight lines, spaced five yards apart. They wore helmets, but no pads yet—her dad had explained that the first few days of practice, they all had to get used to the heat. Two days with helmets, two days with helmets and some pads, and then full pads going forward.

The captains led the team through dynamic stretching. Step forward with one foot. Bend arms and raise above the head. Turn the torso. Arch the back. Next foot forward.

It was like ballet, except with football helmets and very large guys. And no tutus.

She counted four—no, five—no, *six*!—other coaches: her dad's assistants. That was a lot of coaches. Coach had explained their roles— defensive coordinator, defensive line coach, running backs and defensive backs coach, quarterbacks coach . . . she couldn't remember the rest. Coach had mentioned that one of them, Byron Hardy, the defensive coordinator, was a single dad with two little kids.

She had seen them arrive; the kids were cute. They looked like they were about four and six years old. They were sitting near the locker room door, coloring with crayons. Ava loved little kids. She felt comfortable being goofy around them. Not quiet and reserved the way she was at school, and sometimes with kids her own age.

Ava turned her attention back to the field.

She had to make sure her dad's practice was running smoothly. She wanted to assess the way the players and fellow coaches felt about him. Sure he was from Texas originally, but maybe they still saw him as an outsider, an untested guy from a fancy private school in New England.

Her gaze moved to the stands across the field. They were dotted with spectators. Not filled or anything, but a considerable number of people had shown up to watch practice. Were they all parents? She didn't know. Several people had clipboards in their laps, and Ava noticed them jotting things down from time to time. Were they taking notes on her dad's practice? She felt a stab of concern. Was Coach being judged on his very first day?

She heard voices a few rows down from where she was sitting and noticed a group of boys—about her age, it appeared—who must have just gotten there. What were *they* doing here?

Just then, two players jogged onto the field from the locker room. *Uh-oh,* she thought, glancing at the clock. They were twenty minutes late to practice. This was not going to go over well. It was the first day, and Ava knew Coach had to make an example of them.

Her dad blew the whistle and beckoned the players over. She could tell by his stance that he was not happy with their excuse.

She heard one of the boys sitting near her say "Coach Sackett," and her ears pricked up. What were they saying about her dad? She inched over in her seat *ever* so slowly to get into better eavesdropping range.

"—Tyler Whitley," one of the boys was saying.

Oh. So one of the late arrivals was Tyler, the star receiver she'd been hearing about.

"He's only six foot one, but I heard he has a thirty-one-inch vertical leap!" said another kid. "And he runs a four point forty-eight second forty-yard dash!"

"I heard it was four point forty-five!" said a kid with reddish hair. His hair wasn't bright red the way Charlie's was, back home. She loved Charlie's hair. Plus, it was nice to be friends with someone who had as many freckles as she did, not counting Alex.

"Last season PJ threw for five hundred yards and four touchdown passes in that one game against Culver."

Hmm, Ava mused. So the other late arrival was the other star of the team, PJ Kelly. The quarterback. Tommy was a quarterback too. He'd been a star on his team back in Massachusetts, but here in Texas it looked like he might be backup to PJ's backup. She wondered how much that bothered him—or bothered Coach, for that matter.

Ava watched Coach point to the end line. He was going to make Tyler and PJ run sprints for being late. That was standard coaching procedure, of course. Surely everyone in the stands understood that. But Ava was worried. Why did they have to be late on the first day of her dad's practice?

"My dad says Sackett is an unknown," said one of the boys. "And he probably doesn't get what Texas football is like."

Ava felt herself flush with indignation. Her dad was *from* here! He'd only moved to the East Coast to play college ball, and then he'd met her mom, so he stayed. She felt the urge to get up and storm over to these boys. She'd tell them they had no idea what they were talking about. But she knew she could learn more by listening.

"I heard that if the coach doesn't win—and win big—he's out of here. No second chances in Ashland."

That came from the reddish-haired boy. By now Ava was fuming. She clenched her fists and glared at the boy. How *dare* that kid say that about her dad! Who did he think he was? She took a mental snapshot of the boy's face, which she could see only in profile, and vowed to dislike him for the rest of eternity.

"Hi!" said a shy voice on her other side. She turned. Coach Byron's kids were standing next to her. The younger one, the girl, held a pink rubber ball.

The boy smiled at her encouragingly. "Want to play catch?"

Ava pushed aside thoughts about the reddish-haired boy and how much she didn't like him. She hopped up and smiled at the two kids. "I'd love to!" she said.

Later that morning, Alex was sitting at her mom's computer in the living room when Ava, Tommy, and their dad traipsed in from practice. Tommy had on eye black—the stuff players put below their eyes to cut down on glare from the sun—and it was weeping down his cheeks. His face was still flushed with heat and exertion. Her dad wasn't smiling. Even Ava looked uneasy.

"Hi, guys!" Alex chirped brightly anyway. She clapped the computer closed and hopped up from her chair. "Mom found the griddle. She's going to make grilled tomato and cheese sandwiches for lunch. And we finished the first coat of paint in my bedroom! I have to sleep on the couch tonight because of the paint smell. I looked it up: The paint fumes contain harmful chemicals such as solvents and volatile organic compounds, which when inhaled in large quantities can damage the central nervous system."

"That sounds great, honey," said her dad, making his way toward the kitchen.

Tommy didn't say anything, but he tromped heavily up the stairs. A minute later, they heard the shower going.

"What's going on?" Alex asked Ava. "Did the first practice go badly?"

Ava nodded. "It was rough," she said. "They did a lot of running. And also, I think they're both really stressed. Tommy's stressed because suddenly he's just a regular player, not the best. Coach is stressed because a couple of players were late—star players. So he made them run sprints, and I guess you're not supposed to make PJ Kelly and Tyler Whitley run sprints. I hope people understand why Coach did. I hope it will be okay."

"I'm sure it will," said Alex confidently. Her dad was beloved by everyone at their old school. She was sure people here would love him too. "Daddy knows what he's doing."

Upstairs, they heard the shower stop, and a minute or so later, the sound of Tommy playing his keyboard in his room. He loved to play piano—he said sometimes it helped him relieve stress more than football did.

Alex and Ava exchanged a look.

CHAPTER FOUR

Lunch was a glum affair. Tommy ate two grilled cheese sandwiches, and then proceeded to make himself a huge, open-faced turkey sandwich, muttering about needing more protein. Ava wondered how upset he was about not being the star quarterback anymore. After watching him at practice, she had a funny feeling that he didn't mind all that much. Maybe that was the source of the tension between Tommy and Coach. Maybe Tommy could feel Coach's disappointment that he wasn't excited enough about football.

After the lunch dishes were done, Tommy and Coach headed back to the high school for a "chalk and talk" session with the team before the afternoon practice.

Alex went upstairs to map out exactly where she wanted to put her new, supersize bulletin board, which she planned to paint the same color purple as her walls.

Ava couldn't stand being inside another minute. She laced up her high-tops, picked up her basketball, grabbed her bike helmet, and headed outside.

The early afternoon heat enveloped her like a warm bath as she stepped out, but once she'd gotten used to it, she decided it wasn't as bad as it had seemed the day before. Maybe she was becoming a Texan after all.

She bungee-corded her ball onto the rack on the back of her bike (Tommy had helped her set up the rack specifically for that purpose) and pedaled off toward a small park area she'd discovered two blocks from their house.

Her head was hot and itchy inside her bike helmet. For the zillionth time she wished she had a pair of scissors to cut all her hair off.

She pulled up alongside the little park and hopped off. There was no one else here—because who would be dumb enough to want to play outside in this suffocating midday heat?

As she stepped onto the court, the heat rose

up, engulfing her, and she smelled the hot rubber. It was a nice court. Springy surface, level rims; they even had real nets, which her neighborhood park back home hadn't had. She started in close, working the Mikan drill—alternating shooting off her left and right foot—which Tommy had taught her. He was one of these amazing all-around athletes, good at every sport he played. If he kept growing, he could be a legit basketball prospect on top of being a good quarterback. She hoped she would be just like him someday.

"Mind if I shoot around with you?" asked a voice behind her.

She turned.

It was a boy, around her age. A cute boy. He was about her height, with a lanky build and jet-black hair.

In answer, Ava bounce-passed the ball to him. He took a few steps closer to the basket and shot. It didn't go in, but Ava knew enough about basketball to know that he had major skills. She rebounded and bounced it back to him. This time he made it. And then he made the next shot, and the next, and the next.

"I'm Jack," he said, holding onto the ball. "Jack Valdeavano."

Ava raised her eyebrows.

"I know," he said. "It's kind of a mouthful." He smiled. His teeth were bright white against his light-brown skin.

Ava felt herself flushing and hoped it would pass as mere exertion.

"My dad is Mexican," he said. "Which explains my name."

"I'm Ava," she said. She was about to tell him her whole name, but stopped. Maybe this time she'd just be Ava, so she wouldn't have to deal with that now-familiar look when she said the name Sackett. She was also glad that Alex wasn't around. Not because she didn't want her around—it was just that it would be obvious they were twins, and everyone in this town seemed to know that Coach Sackett had identical twin daughters.

"You go to Ashland Middle?" he asked, wrinkling his brow as though trying to place her.

"Um, yeah. At least, I *will* be going. I'm new."

He bounce-passed the ball to her, and she swished it. She moved around the semicircle, making each shot as he passed it to her, happy that she'd found her rhythm at just the right time. Not that she was trying to impress this boy or anything. He *was* pretty good-looking, and she liked the way he smiled sort of crookedly, but she had only just left her kind-of, sort-of crush Charlie behind in Massachusetts. On the other hand, she reflected, she and Charlie hadn't officially been going out or anything.

They played H-O-R-S-E, and Ava beat him by just one letter and with a pretty lucky reverse-hook shot. Then they played one-on-one and Jack beat her, but it was a close game.

"Guess I'd better get going," she said finally, still panting. She realized she'd left the house without water. That was something she'd have to learn not to do when it was this hot outside.

Jack nodded and jogged over to where he'd dropped his backpack. Unzipping it, he pulled out two water bottles and handed her one. "Here," he said. "You look like you could use this."

She gulped it down gratefully and smiled. "Thanks," she said, wiping her mouth with the back of her hand.

"You going to try out for the basketball team?" he asked.

"Not sure," she said, still panting.

"You should. You're good."

She felt herself flush deeper. "Thanks. Oh,

and by the way, my name's Ava Sackett."

"I know," he said simply.

Her eyes widened. "You do? How? Am I that recognizable?"

He shrugged his backpack onto his shoulders. "Nah, your name is on your ball. See you around. Thanks for the game."

She watched him lope off across the park toward the opposite entrance.

"So wait. Does this guy Jack live in our neighborhood?"

It was later that evening. Ava and Alex were sprawled end-to-end across the couch, watching their favorite show, *That's So Awesome!* just like old times. Moxy had leaped onto the couch and contently nestled between them, with the understanding that if Mrs. Sackett should happen to come in, Moxy would jump to the floor in a hurry.

Alex had been so happy when Ava suggested they watch together. They'd been watching the show every week since they were eight or nine years old. It was a little babyish now, they both agreed, but it was their guilty pleasure, something they shared. Alex had been worried that Ava wouldn't want to maintain their silly traditions in the new house.

Ava popped some popcorn into her mouth and chewed it thoughtfully. "He must live around here," she said. "I mean, he was on foot. He wasn't on a bike or anything."

"Hmm," said Alex. "I don't recall seeing his name in the student government at AMS."

"He didn't strike me as the type to run for office," said Ava with a wry smile.

Ava's slight sarcasm went right over Alex's head. "So, do you *like* like him?"

"Oh, no," said Ava. "We just played basketball, that's all."

Alex waited. She knew her sister well enough to recognize the signs of a possible crush.

"Well, okay, so he's a little bit cute. But whatever. We just played ball," said Ava. She appeared to be engrossed in a commercial for breath mints.

Alex grinned. Her sister had a crush! Aside from Charlie, back home, who barely counted because they'd known him since they were all in diapers together, she'd never known her shy, reserved sister to have a real crush. She was giddy with happiness for Ava.

"So how's your student government takeover plan going?" asked Ava, who seemed eager to change the subject.

"Okay, I guess," said Alex. She thought she detected a slight hint of mockery in Ava's tone, but she was never sure. "I've got the chart all done. I've cross-referenced the people in the top positions from last year with sports, clubs, and activities they participated in. It's all available on the password-protected website. I got my registration done yesterday—one more thing to check off my list! Maybe you should register too."

Sometimes Alex's words tumbled out so fast that Ava was the only one who understood her. Ava grinned. "Al. There are still three weeks before school starts. I'll get to it."

"Ave, would it kill you to do things in a timely fashion, rather than waiting till the last minute for everything? Maybe it might help you to be a little more organized when school starts."

Ava glared at her. "Thanks for the tip," she said drily.

Alex hadn't meant to lecture her. But her sister was constantly losing stuff, signing up late, missing deadlines. She always hated it when a teacher called Ava out on a missing assignment. She usually jumped in with some well-thought-out excuse, like that they only had one computer and she, Alex, had spent all night using it so Ava wasn't able to research ancient Mayan culture.

"I'm just trying to help you avoid the usual mad scramble before school starts," she said in a slightly wounded tone. She knew she should stop pressing Ava, but she couldn't help it. "Have you started the books for summer reading?" She was pretty sure she knew the answer to that question. They'd been assigned two books, *To Kill a Mockingbird* and *Call of the Wild*, which of course Alex had long since finished. Alex didn't understand why Ava didn't like to tear through books like she did, but Ava always said she got too distracted and could never stick with a book all the way to the end.

"Al, I'll get it done. I always do," said Ava. "Well, almost always," she added. "Anyway, don't you think you're going a little overboard preparing for the school year? It's still summer!"

"What?" Alex was taken aback.

"I mean, with this whole class president thing—we just moved here! Don't you think you should, you know, wait and see how things work at Ashland Middle School before you charge in there, thinking you've got it all figured out?"

Here Alex had been worrying on Ava's behalf, and now Ava was telling her *she* was the one to be worried about? "So you don't think I can do it? Be class president?" asked Alex.

"Al, I didn't mean it that way," she said.

Alex knew Ava meant well. But her words still stung.

Neither girl said much else until their mom called that it was time for bed.

That night Alex slept on the couch. She wished Ava had invited her to sleep in her room—she had wished that before her own room was filled with toxic paint fumes—but she guessed Ava thought that was too babyish.

CHAPTER FIVE

The next morning the twins were surprised to find their dad at the breakfast table, scribbling down notes on a clipboard.

"Why aren't you at practice?" Ava asked him worriedly. "It's almost eight."

He looked up from his clipboard. "What? Oh. The players are getting weighed and measured and having body comps done. Timed sprints, vertical leaps, that kind of thing. My assistants are handling that. They told me the guys would be too nervous if I were there watching them. Practice doesn't start for another half an hour, but I'm about to head out." He grinned at Ava. "Worried I'd gotten sacked already?"

"What?" said Ava. "No! Of course not." But

she was secretly relieved. "Can I come along?"

"Sure," said their dad.

"No!" said their mom, who had just walked into the kitchen from outside, with Moxy on a leash. She gave Coach a look as she unclipped the leash and picked up Moxy's water dish to refill. "Michael, I'm taking the girls shopping for school clothes today, remember?"

Alex whooped.

Ava groaned.

"Right. Sorry I forgot about that, honey," said Coach. "I've had a lot on my mind."

Mrs. Sackett nodded. "I know," she said. She turned to the girls. "*And* you both need back-to-school haircuts. I made appointments at the salon in the mall."

"Maybe I'll get a full inch trimmed off this time," mused Alex, pulling a tendril of glossy hair around from the side of her head to examine it with pursed lips. "The Texas heat is wreaking havoc on my ends."

"Maybe I'll get it all cut off," said Ava. "It'd be so much easier to deal with in this heat."

"Oh yeah, as if," scoffed Alex. "Why not just dye it blue and get a Mohawk?"

"Maybe I will," retorted Ava. "What do you

think about a blue Mohawk for me, Coach?"

"What?" said their dad, looking up from his practice plan. "Yes. Sounds great."

Ava scowled.

Mrs. Sackett frowned.

"Why can't I go with Coach to practice?" asked Ava, reaching across the table for the box of cereal. "I don't need new clothes. I already have plenty."

Alex buried her face in her hands and shook her head in despair. Then she parted her hands and stared at her sister across the breakfast table. "You just said that to annoy me, didn't you?"

Ava grinned and shrugged. "Maybe. But you know me, Al. My idea of getting dressed up is a clean football jersey."

"Well, *I'm* ready to go shopping," said Alex. She took out her phone and pulled up her list, which was complete with links to different stores' websites.

Ava smiled. "I hope that's in alphabetical order," she teased. She was happy to be joking around with Alex; it meant that things were all right with them again.

Their dad looked up from his clipboard again and stared at his daughters over his half-glasses.

"Go to the mall with your sister, Ave," he commanded. "It will be good for you two to see more
of this town."

"Can I get a new pair of kicking shoes?" Ava
asked eagerly. "My feet have grown, like, half a
size in the past three months."

Their dad exchanged a quick look with their
mom. Then he grumbled under his breath and
looked back down at his clipboard.

Ava bounced in her chair. That meant yes!

"Shotgun!" Ava called as she walked out the
front door toward their mom's red SUV.

"Ugh! Not fair!" cried Alex. "You always get to
sit in front!"

"Because I'm better at Shotgun," Ava said
matter-of-factly. Alex muttered something about
Ava just having better reflexes as she climbed
grudgingly into the backseat.

"We're not in Massachusetts anymore," said
Ava, staring at the houses in their subdivision as
they drove through. "I think I just saw a cactus
in someone's front yard. An *actual* cactus."

"What did you expect? A polar bear?" said

Alex without looking up. She was studying a map of the mall on her smartphone, strategizing the most efficient shopping route.

They passed the little park where Ava had met Jack the day before. Ava thought about him for the hundredth time. He did have a nice smile. She hadn't even asked him what grade he was going into, or what his fall sport was. It was probably football. She wondered if he liked soccer. Here in Texas, people played soccer as a spring sport, so it wouldn't interfere with football. But on the other hand, they were almost as crazy about baseball as they were about football—at least that's what Charlie had told her.

They turned onto a busy four-lane road, flanked with car dealerships and fast-food places. And then they were out of the bustle and Ava stared across vast, flat fields, filled with the same greenish-brown, wispy vegetation. Far off on the horizon, she could see an oil rig silhouetted against the morning sun.

"Have you found the public radio station?" Mrs. Sackett asked Ava. "I haven't unpacked the kitchen radio yet. It feels like days since I've heard any news headlines."

Ava fiddled with the dial. "I think it's all country

music," she said. "Unless you want sports talk."

Mrs. Sackett shuddered. "I think we'll be hearing quite enough of that, too."

The mall loomed up on the left.

"Everything is bigger in Texas," said their mother when she turned into the huge parking lot.

"I heard there's an amazing art supply store here," their mother said, as the three of them stepped into a huge atrium. It was delightfully cool, and classical music was playing.

They all stopped and stared upward at the two-story vaulted ceiling. Even Ava was impressed, although she was aware that people were staring at them. *We might as well have a neon sign over our heads that says "New in Town."*

"Why don't you go to the art store while we head to Spruce?" Alex said to their mom. She was lucky her favorite clothing store had shops in Texas. "You can come meet us when you're done. We'll be there awhile—I have a lot of fashion research to do."

Ava groaned. "Can I go look at shoes at the sports store?"

Mrs. Sackett shook her head. "Not if you don't have your phone with you. Do you have it?"

Ava hung her head. "I just misplaced it."

"Again," said Alex.

"I'll find it. It's probably in my room some-where."

"All right, then I want you girls to stay together," said Mrs. Sackett. "I'll meet you at Spruce in half an hour." She shot Ava a look, which Ava knew meant *Take this one for the team*. Ava sighed and resigned herself to a long morning.

"Spruce is this way," said Alex, looking up from her phone. Ava followed her sister toler-antly through the mall.

They passed an older couple. Ava saw them abruptly stop talking to each other in order to stare at the twins.

"Hey, Al?" said Ava, tugging at her sister's T-shirt. "Alex!" she hissed more urgently.

Alex had been looking over her shopping list but looked up when she heard her sister's tone. "What's up?"

"Have you noticed people . . . staring at us?"

Alex furrowed her brow and scanned the passing shoppers. "No. *Are* they? Why would they stare at *us*?"

Ava shrugged. "No idea. I mean, I'm starting to get why they stare at Coach. They're all obsessed with finding out what he plans to do with the team. But they have no clue who *we* are. Look! See? That guy over there, near the fountain. He just pointed at us and said something to his wife. It's weird."

"You're just imagining things," said Alex. "It's because you hate malls so much. Come on. I just saw some girls our age wearing the cutest outfits, and they were heading into Spruce. Let's follow them and see what they buy. Our school colors are blue and orange. That's kind of hard to work with, but I'm going to try to find some wardrobe basics in those colors."

Suddenly Ava stopped. Alex heard her sharp intake of breath and turned to follow her gaze.

It was a boy with dark hair and an athletic build. He was heading in the direction of the food court and didn't appear to have seen them.

Alex nudged her sister. "Who's that?"

"Who? Oh. Him? No one. Well, okay, it's Jack. The kid I played basketball with yesterday."

Alex craned her neck to take a closer look before Jack was swallowed up in the crowd of shoppers. "He's cute," she pronounced.

Ava shrugged. "I guess."

By that time they had lost sight of the group of girls they'd seen heading into the store, but when they walked in, Alex quickly became focused on the latest fall displays. It wasn't long before she was heading into the dressing room with an armload of clothes to try on.

Ava drifted from one carousel display of clothes to the next, fingering a shirt here, a skirt there, but she didn't see anything she felt like trying on. She definitely needed some new jeans. Hers were getting too small on her. And a new bathing suit, but they were so boring to try on. She wished she had her sister's focus, her ability to zero in on a goal. Maybe that's why teachers all seemed to like Alex but were exasperated by Ava. Ava *meant* to focus, to pay attention. But she was always distracted.

She moved toward the dressing room to find Alex, just as her sister stepped out in a cute white eyelet top over skinny navy-blue shorts. She did a little pirouette in front of the mirror.

"What do you think?" she asked Ava.

"It's pretty," said Ava.

Thankfully, there was a chair at the entrance to the dressing room. Ava sat down wearily as her sister tried on outfit after outfit.

"I'm ready," said Alex at last, emerging in the mint-green ruffled shirt and yellow shorts she had been wearing with a huge pile of clothes draped over her arm. "Mom just texted to say she's on her way. I need to prepare my defense for why I need each of these items."

As they approached the register, Ava heard a flurry of whispering behind her. She turned.

It was the group of girls they'd seen before. One of them stepped forward. "I just figured out who y'all must be!" said a tall girl with straight blond hair. "Aren't you the Sackett twins?"

"Yes!" said Alex eagerly.

Ava was rattled.

"How did you know who we were?" asked Alex.

The other girls tittered. The blond girl opened her phone and sent a quick text. Then she smiled. "The whole town is waiting to meet you. Haven't you noticed how football-crazy everyone is? Your daddy's the main attraction! I'm Emily Campbell, by the way. And this is Annelise and Rosa."

Ava and Alex introduced themselves, just as Mrs. Sackett appeared. They introduced their mother, too.

"I'm sorry to do this, Mrs. Sackett," said Emily, "but my dad just arrived to drive us home, and I told him I'd met y'all. He's parking the car and coming inside to say hello."

"Well, isn't that nice," said Mrs. Sackett, glancing quickly at her watch. "This is such a friendly town!"

"As I'm sure he'll inform you, he used to run the fifty in four point seven seconds, so he should be here very soon. Oh, here he is now."

A man was running through the mall toward them, weaving between shoppers. He skidded to a stop at the front of the store, pivoted quickly like a wide receiver in the open field putting a fake on his defender, and then trotted toward them, thrusting out a huge hand.

"Howdy, ma'am! Bob Campbell!" said Emily's father. He whipped off his hat and shook Mrs. Sackett's hand, still panting slightly. "It's an honor to meet you and your lovely daughters!"

"How nice that our girls have met one another before school starts!" said their mom.

"So tell me, Mrs. Sackett—," said Mr. Campbell.

"Oh, please call me Laura!"

"All right, then, Laura," he said, his grin widening. "So tell me, Laura. How's the team looking?"

She smiled. "Well, they just started practice yesterday. Michael is certainly focusing a lot of energy on it," she said. "It seems to be all he thinks about right now!" She laughed.

Mr. Campbell laughed heartily. Then his face turned serious. He leaned in and spoke to Mrs. Sackett. "I hear he likes to throw the smash concept versus a two high shell," he said in a conspiratorial tone, "but what's his favorite route against a one high safety look?"

"He . . . safety . . . uh, sorry?" asked Mrs. Sackett, looking flustered.

Ava and Alex exchanged a quick glance.

"Aw, Daddy, not now!" pleaded Emily, looking at the twins apologetically.

"And how does he plan to stop Lewisville's spread passing attack?" Mr. Campbell continued. "Against their ten personnel, I imagine he's planning to bring in a nickel corner and add boundary pressure with a fire-zone blitz. Right?"

"What is he *talking* about?" hissed Alex in Ava's ear.

"I barely know!" Ava hissed back. "So Mom has no clue. Look at her face!"

Emily jumped in. "Daddy!" she said, drawing the word out in an exasperated, singsong voice.

"Leave them alone! There'll be plenty of time for you to interrogate Coach Sackett without torturing his family, too!"

Mrs. Sackett laughed weakly, but Ava and Alex could see she was shaken. As were they.

As soon as Mr. Campbell and the girls had left, their mother's smile vanished. "Poor Michael," she murmured, steering Alex toward the register.

Alex's brow furrowed. "Why poor Daddy? Isn't it a good thing that everyone is so interested in his team?"

Her mother pressed her lips together. "Maybe. But he's under a lot of pressure to do well. Although he *did* warn me, I hadn't quite realized the depth of people's passion for this sport." Then she noticed the pile of clothes Alex was holding and frowned.

"Since you guys have all these clothes to argue about, can I go to the sports store and meet you at the haircut place?" Ava pleaded.

"This *is* a very large selection, Alex," their mom said. "Surely you don't think I'm going to buy all of it?"

Alex smiled at their mother. "I was assuming we were just going to begin the process of negotiations."

"I'll meet you guys at the salon," said Ava, suppressing a smile.

"All right, but your appointments are in twenty minutes. And Ave, we *have* to get you some school stuff," her mother called after her. "You *can't* wear football jerseys every day."

"Sure I can," said Ava. "There's no dress code at Ashland Middle, remember? It's a public school! No more collared shirts and skirts to iron like at Randall Prep!" Ava grinned and waved to them over her shoulder as she headed out of Spruce and toward the sporting-goods store.

After much discussion, Mrs. Sackett made some of Alex's purchases, and then the two headed toward the hair salon. Mrs. Sackett chatted about the art supply store and how pleasantly surprised she'd been to find some of her favorite paint brands. Then they passed the food court and Alex did a double take.

Jack. Ava's crush. He was easily recognizable in his orange basketball jersey, with his jet-black hair. He was sitting at a table with someone.

A girl.

Alex moved behind a potted palm, which was conveniently located outside the food court. She peered through the leaves. There was no mistaking the body language between Jack and the girl. The situation had "date" written all over it. She watched them laughing about something. She didn't like the looks of the girl. She was certainly pretty, with blond hair, a slender build, and candy-pink nails. The girl reached over and helped herself to one of Jack's french fries. *Ew.* Way too flirty.

"Al, what are you doing?" asked her mother. "We'll be late for the hair appointment."

Alex stepped away from her surveillance position and rejoined her mother. But she was lost in thought. She wondered how much Ava really liked Jack. *Poor Ave,* she thought. *Her second-ever crush, and he already has a girlfriend.* Her sister was headed for certain disappointment. It was hard not to get mad at Jack. What was he up to, flirting with Ava? She'd need to talk Ava out of liking him and find someone more appropriate for her.

CHAPTER SIX

Ava was at the salon waiting for them when they arrived. The place was bustling. Ava and Alex were both given gowns to put on and then led to stations on opposite sides of the center aisle of mirrors. Mrs. Sackett settled into an empty chair along the wall behind Alex and opened her mystery novel.

Alex's stylist was named Jolene. She was young, with shoulder-length, butter-colored hair that gleamed in the salon's flattering lighting. Soon she and Alex were chatting away.

"I was thinking of maybe adding in some layers," said Alex. She looked at Jolene in the mirror for confirmation. "Or straightening it?"

"I don't think you need layers," said Jolene,

fluffing up Alex's hair with all ten fingers. She sectioned off a horizontal part and twisted the rest of Alex's hair into a ponytail. Then she secured it with a clip to the top of her head. "And you've got such a fantastic natural curl. It'd be a shame to see it go." Her silver scissors flashed as she snipped away.

"What about highlights?" asked Alex. "It seems like a lot of the girls at my new school have blond hair. Should I lighten my hair up, do you think? Nothing too crazy, maybe just some caramel-colored pieces . . . it can be kind of a gradual transition and then maybe I can go lighter. . . ." Alex chattered on.

"Stop!" said Jolene, laughing. "Dark hair and green eyes—why, you have Scarlett O'Hara's coloring!"

Alex knew that was a character from *Gone with the Wind*. She made a mental note to add the book to her reading list.

"Anyway, didn't I see you with a twin sister?" asked Jolene. "How silly would it look for you to have blond hair when your identical twin doesn't?"

"That's true," said Alex. "And of course I would *never* change my look drastically without consulting Ava. We've always had the same hairstyle. I just want to be sure I'm up-to-date with whatever is trending at my new school. I've noticed everyone here seems to have straight hair. Are you sure my curls aren't a problem?"

Jolene laughed again. "You're a beautiful girl with beautiful hair. And clearly very smart, too! I wouldn't be too worried."

They talked about nail color and fashions, Jolene's scissors flashing and whirring all the while as a small fringe of brown hair fell to the floor around Alex's chair.

At last she handed Alex a mirror and spun her around so she could see the back.

"Thanks. It looks great," said Alex. "You like it, Mom?"

Her mom didn't answer. Alex put the hand mirror down and looked at her mother. Didn't she like her hair?

But Mrs. Sackett wasn't staring at Alex. She was staring past her. Alex swiveled her chair around to follow her gaze.

Ava had emerged from around the bank of mirrors. She stood a few feet away, still draped in her navy-blue smock, smiling shyly at them.

Alex gasped.

Ava's hair was all cut off. Up to her *chin*. It was almost as short as *Tommy's*. For a second or two, Alex thought maybe it was just pulled back in a bun, although logically that made no sense. Then the realization sank in.

"What did you do?" sputtered Alex.

Jolene seemed to sense that now might be a good time to step away. "You're all set, honey," she said, patting Alex on the shoulder. "I have another client." She turned meaningfully toward Mrs. Sackett. "Good luck with them, Mom," she said, and hurried off.

Ava's smile had evaporated. "You don't like it?"

Actually, now that the initial shock was wearing off, Alex had to admit, objectively, that she *did* like it. The shorter hair brought attention to Ava's great cheekbones—cheekbones Alex realized she must have too, but somehow had never noticed. Ava looked delicate and pretty, adorable but totally sophisticated. And *completely different*. Alex didn't know whether to feel upset or jealous. But she definitely felt betrayed.

"No!" said Alex. "I mean, yes! I mean, you just look so . . . different! Why didn't you . . . ask me? Why'd you just do it?" Alex didn't mean for her words to come out so forcefully, but she couldn't help it.

Ava's brow furrowed. "I didn't *know* I needed your per*mission*," she said with some heat. "I did it for sports. I'm so sick of dealing with hot, sweaty hair all the time. It's so much easier like this."

Mrs. Sackett stood up and went to Ava, wrapping an arm protectively around her shoulder. *Why is she comforting Ava right now?* Alex thought bitterly. She, Alex, was the one who needed comforting. This was totally catastrophic. No—*cataclysmic.* That was the word for it.

"Well," sniffed Ava. "Obviously you don't like it. Sorry if you're embarrassed to be seen with me."

"That's not fair," said Alex, her voice quivering. She wanted to say so much more, to explain to her sister that her reaction had nothing to do with embarrassment and everything to do with feeling abandoned, but she was afraid she'd cry, and that would be mortifying in the middle of the salon.

"I think you look wonderful, pumpkin," said her mother hastily. She spun Ava around to face her, crooked her index finger under Ava's chin, and tilted her face up slightly, the better to admire her new look. "I had no idea curly hair could look this cute short, but this haircut is just so becoming on you!"

As Alex had said to Jolene, she and Ava had had the same hairstyles their whole lives. Back when they were six, they'd both gotten bobbed to just an inch or so below the chin. That had been the shortest they'd ever gone. And they'd done it together. It wasn't about how short Ava's hair was—although it was *very* short, in Alex's opinion—it was just that Ava had chosen such a dramatic way to emphasize how far apart they were growing. Was this Ava's way of announcing that she no longer wanted to look like twins?

That night Alex slept on the couch again. Before she went to sleep, she sorted through her final choices of bulletin-board pictures. She came upon a picture of herself and Ava, grinning from the side of a swimming pool, their chins on their arms, their elbows side by side. They were both missing their two front teeth, and they both had their hair slicked back. They were about seven years old, she guessed. And they looked absolutely, positively identical. She sighed and placed the photo in the "do not put up" pile.

Then she burrowed into the couch cushions and held her half of the baby blanket tight. Once again, she wished Ava had invited her to sleep in her room tonight. Obviously Ava was trying to look forward, rather than back. Well, maybe she was right. And if looking forward was what Ava was going to do, then maybe Alex ought to do the same thing.

Upstairs in her room, Ava wasn't asleep either. She was thinking about Alex and wishing Alex had asked to sleep in her room tonight. But Alex hadn't asked. She'd seemed to prefer the couch. *Oh well.* Just another example of how they were growing apart.

Ava ran a hand through her short hair for the zillionth time. She still couldn't believe she'd gone through with it, despite having threatened to every day since they'd moved to Texas. It bothered her that Alex was pretending to be shocked about it. Granted, she hadn't exactly *discussed* her decision with her sister, but she'd made it clear plenty of times that she wanted to cut her hair. And besides, just because her hair was short didn't make it all that different. It was still brown and curly like Alex's. There was just less of it now.

No, that wasn't what Alex was upset about, Ava decided. She was just upset because she thought it didn't look good. Or maybe Alex thought short hair was hopelessly uncool, and that Ava had forfeited any chance of becoming accepted into the popular crowd. Well, so what? It was exhausting, trying to fit in. She'd always had Alex, and Charlie. Charlie wouldn't care about a stupid haircut.

Her mind wandered to Jack. She wondered if he would like it. Then she reprimanded herself. She barely knew the guy. He probably had a girlfriend. No one that good-looking and that athletic would be single. Right?

Her phone vibrated. She'd found it, of course, when they had gotten home from the mall. It had slipped behind her bed. She did lose stuff a lot, but she always found it again, eventually. The problem last year had been that the things she tended to misplace were usually homework assignments. And handing homework in the next day usually resulted in a lower grade. She sighed. She really hoped she could do better this year—maybe starting over at a new school would help.

She glanced at her phone. It was a text from Charlie. That was weird. Almost like he sensed her thoughts from so many miles away.

Hey cowboy.
What up?

Not much.
Got all my hair cut off.

Huh. For real?

Yep. It's good for sports.

Send me a pic?

Maybe tomorrow.
It's all sticking up right now.

You playing football?

Not sure yet.
But I played basketball.
Might try out for the team.

Awesome.

Ava knew it was her turn to say something. But she couldn't think of anything to say. She was thinking about Jack. She was even starting to have trouble picturing what Charlie looked like.

She knew Charlie was waiting for her next text, so she added:

> Well, G2G.
> Going to Coach's 6 a.m. practice tomorrow. Ha ha.

CU L8ter 😊

> Yep, talk later.

She turned off her phone. She missed Charlie, but once school started, they'd probably get so busy, they'd forget about staying in touch. Did that bother her? Well, of course. And yet, every time she tried to conjure up what Charlie looked like, Jack's face shimmered into her thoughts instead.

CHAPTER SEVEN

At 5:15 the following morning, Ava's alarm went off. With a groan, she slapped the snooze button. Then she heard the rain outside and groaned again. No way was she going to practice. She turned off her alarm and went back to sleep.

By the time she came down for breakfast, well after nine, the rain had mostly stopped, and Coach and Tommy were already back and showered. The only signs that they'd been out were the dripping ponchos hanging from the corner of the kitchen door.

"Hey, sport," said her dad, who was pouring himself a cup of coffee. Tommy was hunched over a huge plate of scrambled eggs and bacon, shoveling forkfuls in as though he hadn't eaten for three days. Moxy was lying under the kitchen table, waiting hopefully for Tommy to drop a piece of bacon or a lump of egg.

The newspaper was open in front of her father's plate. Ava could see the headline: RETURN-ERS KELLY AND WHITLEY TO ANCHOR SACKETT'S OFFENSE.

"Still can't get used to your hair," said Tommy through a mouthful of eggs.

Ava raked her fingers through her hair. "Me neither. Already I can't get it to look like it did at the salon. But I don't care. I like it."

Tommy nodded and swallowed. "Me too, Ave. I think you look awesome."

Ava beamed. She'd sent Charlie a picture of her haircut this morning, and he'd texted back that he liked it too. She sat down and poured herself some cereal. "Rain's stopped. It feels cooler out there too. Do you guys have time to throw the ball around after breakfast?"

Coach grinned ruefully. "That's like asking a mailman to go for a walk on his day off," he said with a chuckle. Then, noticing the disappointed look on Ava's face, he reached across the table and ruffled her hair. "Sure, I've got some time."

"Me too," said Tommy.

Ava's smile returned. She stood up and grabbed

an apple from the fruit bowl on the counter.

Coach adjusted his half-glasses and frowned as he scanned the article in the paper. "Everyone's a coach," he muttered softly, mostly to himself. "They all think they have the answers."

"Morning!" Alex chirped, bouncing into the kitchen. She was always cheerful in the morning. Moxy's tail thumped under the table.

Ava, who had just bitten into the apple, looked up at her sister and stopped mid-chew.

Alex had straightened her hair. It swung and bounced around her shoulders as she flounced over to their dad and kissed him on the cheek.

Mrs. Sackett came into the kitchen, carrying a basket of clean laundry. She stopped in the doorway and gaped at Alex. "Sweetie! Your hair! How—how—um, straight it looks!"

Alex flipped her hair back and smiled. "Thanks," she said. "I'm experimenting a little."

"Great," said Tommy. "Now you look like every other girl in Ashland. What is it with straight hair, anyway?"

"It's the style now," said Alex simply. She got a cereal bowl out of the cupboard.

Ava glowered. Was this Alex's not-so-subtle way of telling her that she, Ava, ought to put

more effort into her own appearance? Ava had
to admit, Alex looked pretty. But she also looked
like every other ordinary pretty girl. Gone were
her glossy curls.

Alex had clearly registered her sister's disap-
proval. She sat down heavily in the chair across
from Ava and poured out some cereal. Then she
placed the box directly in between them, so neither could see the other.

Tommy looked from one sister to the other
with a bemused expression. "Trouble in para-
dise?" he asked.

"Can you ask Ava to hand me a spoon,
please?" asked Alex.

"Ava, can you reach a spoon from the drawer
behind you for your twin sister, Alex?"

Ava got a spoon from the drawer and handed
it to Tommy, who handed it to Alex.

"Tommy, can you ask Alex to please not finish the good cereal?" Ava said from behind the
cereal box.

"Alex, your twin sister, Ava, requests that
you not finish all the good cereal," said Tommy.
He seemed to be enjoying himself.

Coach put down his paper. He looked from
one girl to the other over his half-glasses.

"What's going on with you two?" he asked.

"Nothing," they answered in unison.

"Well, they've still got their creepy twin-speak going," said Tommy with a grin. He stood up. "Come on, Ave. You finished? We'll go out back and you can kick to me."

Ava jumped up. Alex continued to eat her cereal, intently reading the news on her phone.

The phone rang. "I'll get it," said their mom, setting down the basket. She glanced at the empty phone holder and let out an exasperated sigh. "It would be *nice* if someone put the phone *back* in the *cradle* once in a while!" She ran into the other room. "It's in the couch cushion!" they heard her yell, but she answered on the fourth ring, just before it went to voice mail.

Coach set down his newspaper. "Honey, is something going on between you and your sister?" he asked quietly.

"I don't know," Alex replied. "I mean, from my end I don't think so. But everything I do seems to annoy her these days. Or 'antagonize,'" she added. "That's a better word. I don't know what I'm doing to antagonize her."

"I think you ought to talk to her about it," he suggested. "You two never stay mad for long."

Alex nodded. "I guess so. She's also worried about you, and I'm finding her anxiety somewhat infectious."

He put down his paper. "Worried? About me?"

"Yes, she says that people are paying attention to every move you make with the team—that they're all really critical here, and not as friendly as they act."

He patted her hand. "Honey, there's no need for you girls to worry. People are just interested in football. For a lot of folks in this town the Friday night games are the highlight of their week, something to look forward to. They just want to hear about the team, that's all."

Alex nodded, reassured as always by her dad's easygoing confidence.

Mrs. Sackett returned to the kitchen. "That was April Cahill, who lives down the street," she said. "There's a neighborhood block party in two weeks, and we're all invited. I'm glad we have friendly neighbors!"

Coach gave Alex a rueful grin. "Yep. They are mighty friendly."

CHAPTER EIGHT

That afternoon Alex broke her "not talking to Ava" rule by announcing she was coming along with her twin to see their dad's second practice of the day. Ava seemed pleasantly surprised.

The sun had come out, and the rain had cooled things off considerably. Alex felt like things had cooled off a little between her and Ava, too—her hurt and anger had dimmed from a huge flame inside her to more of a flickering light. Plus, she'd felt a twinge of satisfaction seeing the look on Ava's face when she noticed Alex's straight hair; maybe her sister *did* care a little bit about looking different from each other.

"Have you suddenly taken an interest in football?" Ava asked as the two sisters mounted the steep stadium steps a few rows above the team locker room.

"Not exactly," said Alex, pushing a silky strand of straight hair away from her face. "But I realized I haven't seen the high school yet," she continued, settling into her seat and adjusting her fashionable dark sunglasses. "And I should really check it out, since it's right across the parking lot from Ashland Middle School. I saw on the website that the AMS student government has done some joint fund-raisers with AHS, so maybe I can do some networking today. Wow. There are a *ton* of people watching practice." She scanned the bleachers. "Don't they have to go to work and stuff?"

"I guess it's like this every day," said Ava. "They come and sit and watch. Some of them take notes. When Coach yells at PJ or Tyler or even Tommy, I see them whispering to one another, or writing stuff down. It's weird."

Alex looked at Ava over her dark glasses. "Are you still worried about Daddy? He told me there was absolutely nothing to worry about. And haven't you noticed? He's a rock star in this town, from the amount of attention we always get when we go places."

Ava shook her head. "I *am* still worried about him—he's under a lot of pressure. If they lose too many games this season, his job could be in trouble. Plus, I'm hearing people say he's being too harsh with some of the players. I heard that the mother of PJ Kelly, the quarterback, was complaining about Coach to one of the assistants."

"How did you hear that?" asked Alex.

"Shane told me. He's Coach Byron's son. He's only six, but he's doesn't miss much."

Alex furrowed her brow and stared down at the field. Hadn't their dad just told her not to be worried? Now Ava was saying there were a lot of reasons to worry.

Their dad whistled to a kid and called him over. They watched him talking animatedly, waving his arms and pointing.

"That's PJ," said Ava. "See? The other players are talking behind Coach's back. And look at the people in the stands. People don't like it when PJ gets yelled at. What if they're complaining about Coach?"

Alex raised her sunglasses to look, a troubled expression on her face.

The two girls watched the team divide up into its specialty areas and head off with the various coaches. Because it was the third day of practice, the players were now wearing some pads underneath their practice uniforms.

Just then, Alex noticed that four kids were making their way up the stands to where she and Ava were sitting. She couldn't see the ones in the back very well, but the girl in front was Emily, whom they'd met at the mall yesterday.

"Pssst," said Alex to Ava. "Don't look now, but I think that group goes to AMS." She bounced up and down excitedly. "And they look like they're coming over here to talk to us!"

As the group came closer, Alex saw Ava's face light up too. Alex followed her sister's gaze to a dark-haired boy who was bringing up the rear of the group. He grinned at Ava with a cute half smile. *Oh—that's Jack,* Alex realized. She recognized him from yesterday at the mall. When he'd been with his *girlfriend*. She looked at him coolly.

"Hey, y'all!" said Emily. "Oh my gosh, I love your hair, Al—wait, are you Alex or Ava?"

"Ava," she said shyly. "And thanks!"

"Wow, you guys look so different!" Emily said. "Now we'll definitely be able to tell y'all apart!"

Alex kept a bright smile on her face, but she

was fuming inside. She didn't *want* to look different from Ava! And they weren't that hard to tell apart anyway, considering that Ava never wore anything nicer than jeans and a T-shirt.

"I heard you might be at practice today, so I wanted to introduce you to some kids," Emily went on. "This is Jack, and you met Rosa yesterday at the mall. And this is Corey." She gestured to another boy, who had reddish hair.

Alex looked at him for the first time, and all angry thoughts flew out of her head. She couldn't speak. All she could manage was a goofy smile. Corey was tall. Athletic. And heart-stoppingly gorgeous.

Wait, why was Ava nodding so coldly at him?

The girls sat down on either side of Alex and Ava and were soon chatting away. Alex did what she could to join in, but she could feel Corey staring at her. Every time she looked up, he looked hastily away. He and Jack were sitting just in front of them, but they turned around to join the girls' conversation.

"So Ava here is great at basketball," Jack said to Corey, gesturing toward Ava.

Ava's ears turned red. Alex knew her well enough to know this meant she liked Jack. Her heart sank. Well, of course, Ava *was* a good athlete, but Alex could only hear the flattery part. The nerve of the guy! He already had a girlfriend!

Speaking of girlfriends . . . She wondered if Corey had one. He seemed like he could be an ideal boyfriend candidate. She wondered if he was a good student. If so, he really would be perfect!

Then she heard Jack mention Corey's name. She tuned back in.

"Corey plays quarterback for AMS," Jack said. "Although we could totally use him on the basketball team."

Corey shrugged and scuffed a foot. "My older brother just graduated from AHS," he said. "He taught me how to play football. I like to come to AHS practices because I learn a lot." He turned to Alex. "Do *you* like sports?"

Alex still couldn't form words. Why did she have to get so tongue-tied around guys? She had no trouble talking to anyone else! All she could manage was a sort of gulping sound.

Ava jumped in. "Alex was huge on school spirit back at our old school," she informed the group.

Alex finally found her voice. "Yeah, but I

didn't do anything that involved any actual moving. I'm a total klutz athletically," she said. "I think 'ungainly' is a good word to describe me."

Corey laughed. Alex noticed her sister scowl. What was her problem with Corey?

"Ava's the athlete," Alex continued loyally, smiling at her sister. "She's awesome at any sport she tries."

Jack grinned at Ava.

Ava glared at Corey.

Corey was hanging on every word Alex said.

Alex sniffed and turned away from Jack.

Then Emily and Rosa steered the conversation toward school and teachers and classes, and Corey and Jack went to join another group of boys a couple of bleacher sections away. As they headed off, Corey glanced back and almost smashed into a stair railing, catching himself just in time. Alex giggled and then joined the animated conversation with her new friends. Ava, as usual when around new people, was pretty quiet, only speaking when someone asked her a question. Alex tried bringing her into the conversation, but it seemed like Ava's mind was elsewhere. After a while, Alex heard their father calling.

"Girls! Time to head home!"

Alex exchanged phone numbers with the other girls. Ava had forgotten her phone again.

They followed their dad and Tommy toward the car a few minutes later. "Jack's great, huh?" Ava said when they were in the backseat (shotgun rules didn't apply after practice; Tommy automatically got the front).

Alex shrugged. "He's okay. How much do you really *like* like him?" She knew she should say something to her sister about how she'd seen him in the mall that day with the blond girl; how she was 98 percent sure she was his girlfriend. She just couldn't bring herself to deflate Ava's first crush in their new town.

Ava reddened. "I never said I *like* liked him. We just played basketball, that's all."

"Okay," said Alex, deciding to let it drop. "So, what'd you think of Corey?"

"Oh. Corey. Yeah. He's okay," said Ava.

"You don't think he's supercute?"

Ava shrugged.

They were silent for a few minutes, and then Ava blurted out, "You weren't too friendly to Jack."

Alex shrugged. "He's fine," she said carefully. She didn't know what to say! "He just . . . well, he strikes me as a little inappropriate for you."

Ava's eyes narrowed. "Inappropriate? You sound like a teacher, Al. I'm not saying this because I like Jack or anything. I don't. But you were turning your back to him and practically ignoring everything he said. Do you think he's inappropriate because he isn't on the middle school football team, like Corey? Or part of student government? Or just because he's not cool enough?"

Alex was outraged. "No! I never implied that! I just think he—he lacks character. Anyway, you weren't especially friendly to Corey. What was that about?"

Ava shrugged again.

"Maybe *you* like him?" accused Alex.

Ava's eyes widened with horror. "Him? Ew! No!"

Alex's eyes flashed with anger. She thought again about telling Ava that the guy she liked was a double-crossing two-timer. "Scoundrel" was a good word for him. But this time she chose not to out of anger.

By the time they got home, neither girl was speaking to the other.

Again.

CHAPTER NINE

On Saturday afternoon Tommy came home early from practice.

"Is everything okay?" Mrs. Sackett asked him worriedly. "You didn't hurt yourself, did you?"

"Everything's fine," said Tommy. "We had baseline concussion testing today—just a bunch of computer questions that measure our processing speed and reaction time in case we ever get a concussion."

Mrs. Sacket looked relieved. "Got it. Well, I was going to take the girls to the pool. But maybe you'd like to take them?"

"Sure," Tommy said. "I heard some of the guys say they might be heading there too."

It had taken awhile to understand the driving

laws in Texas, but Tommy and their mom had finally gotten the paperwork straightened out saying that it was legal for Tommy to drive his siblings.

The car ride there was quiet. After a few minutes, Tommy gave up trying to find a station that didn't play country. This time Alex had actually won the shotgun battle for the front passenger seat. They rode in silence until Alex finally cleared her throat and blurted out a question.

"How are things between you and Daddy?" she asked Tommy.

Ava perked up her ears.

Tommy drummed the wheel thoughtfully, as though trying to think of the best way to respond. "Things are okay, not great," he said. "Some of the guys think Coach is being really harsh on a few players. Like PJ and Tyler. And even me," he added grimly.

"Oh," said Alex worriedly. "I thought things were better."

In the backseat, Ava crossed her arms and sulked. She'd been concerned about their dad since they'd gotten to Texas. Why had it taken Alex so long to get a clue?

But she knew the answer to that. That was

the way Alex always was: quick to love everyone and see the bright side of everything. She was slow to acknowledge that a person might have ulterior motives and wasn't quite as nice as she thought. Alex liked everyone, and everyone liked Alex.

As they pulled into the parking lot, Tommy put the car in park and then took out his phone to check his texts. "A bunch of guys from the team are meeting up here," he announced. "You girls okay staying awhile?"

"Yes!" said Alex quickly. "I just got a text from Emily. She said she's on her way here too. I guess a whole bunch of AMS kids come to this pool on Saturdays. Let's stay as long as possible." Ava had to admire her sister. She was very good at sizing up the social landscape of a new place and strategically putting herself into the right situations. How had she known that this pool, which was across town from their neighborhood, was the place to see and be seen? *She probably* will *get herself elected class president,* Ava thought.

The girl at the front desk smiled at Tommy. Ava had noticed that girls did this a lot these days. Then the girl looked at the twins, and realization dawned on her face. "Oh! Y'all must be the Sacketts, right?"

"Yeah," said Tommy with a grin. "My twin sisters are a dead giveaway. How much do we owe you?"

"No charge for y'all," she said, waving them through. "Women's locker room on the left, men's is straight ahead."

"Thanks," said Alex and Ava together.

"A girl could get used to this royal treatment," Alex whispered to Ava as they headed into the locker room to change.

The swimming area was enormous. There were three different pools—one shallow wading pool full of little kids and their parents; another, directly in front of them, that looked like a tween and teen hangout; and a third that looked like an Olympic-size pool and was marked off with lanes. Serious swimmers were doing laps, and a swim practice was going on at the far end.

As Tommy headed off to find his teammates, the girls found two empty chairs and dragged them together. Then they laid out their towels. Alex settled into her chair and opened her magazine as Ava peeled off her T-shirt. Her mom had finally convinced her to buy a new bathing suit, and she had to admit, she loved it. It was a sleek, silver, one-piece racer.

Alex, in contrast, had talked their mother into buying her two new suits. Today she was debuting a cute fluorescent-blue bikini with a retro-looking, forties-style halter top.

Ava had just gotten settled into her chair and closed her eyes when she heard Alex squeal.

"There's Emily!"

Alex sat up and waved wildly.

Ava opened one eye. Emily was waving back from the other side of the pool, beckoning to them. Or was it just to Alex? Ava was so accustomed to being friends with Alex's friends. It had always been convenient for quiet, reserved Ava, not having to make small talk and flit around at birthday parties. She usually liked Alex's friends just fine, and they her, but here it seemed like a whole new ball game. Ava hadn't spoken to Emily very much, so she couldn't really assume Emily already wanted to be her friend. Maybe she was just beckoning to Alex.

"Let's go over there," said Alex excitedly.

"Now?" said Ava. "We just got settled here."

"Ave," said Alex in her most matter-of-fact

voice. "This is an important social opportunity for both of us."

Ava sat up and swung her legs around to stand up. "You go ahead," she said to Alex. "I just saw Coach Byron and his kids, Jamila and Shane—the ones we see at practice sometimes. I'm going to go say hi."

"Okay," said Alex. "I'll be over there."

Ava sighed. Playing with younger kids seemed so much less complicated. She just didn't have the energy to delve into the Ashland Middle School social scene. Not yet.

As Alex made her way around the pool, she spotted a boy in the water. He had reddish hair, and he was hanging out at the side of the pool, talking with Emily and her friends, who were sitting on lounge chairs. Was it Corey? Her heart thudded. She could only see him from the back. Water streamed off his shoulders as he pulled himself effortlessly out of the pool and then stood up.

As she approached them, she silently thanked her mother for letting her buy this second bathing suit. She knew she looked great in it.

Corey must have thought so too, because as soon as he caught sight of her he tripped backward over a lounge chair, barely catching himself before he fell into the pool.

Alex giggled. He was truly adorable. Her breath caught in her throat as she noticed how his bright-blue eyes seemed to glow, even from this far away.

"Hey!" he called to her.

"Hi!" she said brightly, addressing the group. She tried not to look at Corey too much, but her eyes seemed drawn to him.

"Don't you look cute as a bug!" said Emily, leaping up and hurrying over to Alex. She crooked her elbow through Alex's and led her to a free chair in the midst of the group. Alex could see Corey out of the corner of her eye as he headed over to a group of his friends and sat down. She was pretty sure he was still gawking at her.

"Where's that twin sister of yours?" asked Rosa, sitting up on one elbow and smiling at Alex.

Alex looked around. She spotted Ava in the kiddie pool, moving through the shallow end with Jamila on her back and Shane chasing them. The kids were screaming with delight.

"Over there," she said, smiling. "She's playing 'shark attack' with those little kids."

"Aw, how sweet," said Annelise. "We were just heading to the snack bar," she went on. "Want to come with us?"

"Oh, thanks, I'm fine for now," Alex said. Then she wondered if that had been a mistake. Should she have agreed to go with them? Had she missed an important socializing opportunity? Or would this be the perfect chance to think of a reason to say something to Corey?

The three girls stood up. Emily smiled at Alex and tossed her a bottle of sunscreen. "Here, slather up," she said. "You northerners need to get used to our Texas sun!"

As Alex was putting sunscreen on her legs, a shadow fell over her. She looked up. It was Corey. Gulp.

"How's it going?" he asked.

"Um, great." She knew she had to say something, but her mind was totally blank.

"So how's your dad's team look?" Corey finally said.

Alex's heart sank. She knew nothing about

football and cared nothing about football. She couldn't carry on a conversation about it to save her life—not like Ava could. She would have to make a note to learn the game better. She could learn the players' names, that kind of thing. But for now, what should she say to Corey? She needed to come up with a standard response to this question, because it seemed to be the one everyone asked.

"Um, okay, I guess," she managed.

Corey abruptly sat down next to her on the lounge chair. Her whole body stiffened—whether in thrilled excitement or pure terror, she had no clue.

"Sorry, that was a dumb question," he said.

"No, it wasn't. It's just that I—"

"You've probably been asked that by every person in this whole town," he said.

She smiled gratefully. "I do hear it a lot," she admitted.

"I was just trying to make conversation. I'm not great at small talk."

Inside, her stomach did a cautious little flip. Maybe he liked her, too!

"Well, you should really ask my sister that question," she said. "She's really into our dad's team. She even plays football herself. She was the star kicker at our school back in Massachusetts."

"No kidding," he said. "That's pretty cool. But you told me before you weren't that into sports, right?"

She nodded. "Yeah, I'm very uncoordinated," she said. "Ava and I are pretty different, even though we look exactly alike. Or used to," she added under her breath.

"It must be awesome to have a twin. You two are probably super close, huh?"

A wave of sadness washed over her. "We always have been," she said. "But since we moved here, we've kind of been drifting apart a little."

"I guess you guys must be under a lot of pressure, just like your dad is," said Corey thoughtfully. "I was just talking about it with my dad last night. He said a lot of people have been kind of ragging on Coach Sackett at practice, criticizing some of his coaching decisions and saying if your dad doesn't get to the state finals, he'll be out of a job. That there are no second chances in Ashland." Seeing Alex's horrified face, he quickly continued. "But my dad said that wasn't fair. People who know what they're talking about, who really know the game, are saying that your dad is an awesome coach. He needs a season to rebuild the team because they lost a lot of seniors and they're not very big this year. I think your dad's awesome. I learn so much about my own game when I watch him coaching."

Alex flashed a dazzling smile. "Thanks for saying that."

His ears instantly turned bright red, which made her like him all the more.

The others returned just then, carrying drinks and snacks and chattering away about the latest episode of a reality TV show Alex hadn't heard of. She told herself she would look into it before school started.

Corey stood up. Over where his friends were sitting, the boys were collecting their towels and clothes and shoving them into backpacks. "Gotta go," he said, a bit wistfully. "Our summer park district football team has practice."

He and Alex exchanged a quick smile. He jerked his chin up ever so slightly as a quick good-bye gesture to her, and she felt herself blush. She was glad she had on her big sunglasses.

Alex watched him knock over a small plastic table as he left. He joined up with his friends and then they all wound their way through the sea of suntanners and swimmers. She sighed. How could anyone be that cute *and* that nice?

An hour or so passed, in which the girls alternated between jumping into the pool and lounging and chatting. Occasionally Alex would wave to Ava, beckoning her to come join them, but each time she was either in the middle of a game or under water. Then Emily glanced at the time on her phone. "We better get going," she said to Rosa and Annelise. "We're all assistant counselors at a cheerleading camp for little kids, which starts next week. We have to go to a meeting. Are you going to try out for the squad this year?"

Alex shook her head quickly. "I really am a klutz," she admitted.

"Oh, nonsense!" said Emily with a tinkling laugh. "How can the coach's daughter not be coordinated?"

Alex laughed too and made a mental note to look into cheerleading. How hard could it be? Her friend Isabel back in Boston was a cheerleader. Maybe she *should* go out for the squad. It definitely seemed like something that could elevate her social status at AMS and make her more of a public figure. "But anyway, I think I need to get going too. I should find Ava and my brother."

The girls left, and Alex stood up to look for Ava.

She scanned the kiddie pool again and spotted her in the far end, blowing up an inflatable beach ball with Coach Byron's kids. Then Alex did a double take. Her gaze shifted to the main pool.

There, in the water right in front of her, was Jack. He was laughing and splashing a girl who had just gotten out of the pool and was toweling off. It was the blond girl from the mall. Alex was sure it was the same person. She looked quickly toward the other pool to see if Ava had spotted them as well, but Ava gave no sign of having seen them.

She thought of calling after Emily to ask her who the girl was, but Emily and the other girls were already heading into the locker room.

She made another mental note, this time to keep a careful eye on that guy. He really had no right to flirt with her sister when he obviously already had a girlfriend.

CHAPTER TEN

"What do you think, honey? Black or beige?"

It was the following Sunday, the day of the block party. Mrs. Sackett stood at the doorway to Alex's room, alternately standing on one foot and then the other, to show Alex the two different sandal choices. Mrs. Sackett was wearing a new sundress she'd bought the day they'd all gone to the mall. It looked pretty on her. Because of her artistic leanings, her mom had an excellent sense of color and what worked well with her complexion. But as for putting an outfit together—she let Alex handle the actual fashion decisions.

Alex pinched her lower lip and frowned, sizing up her mom's outfit. "Beige, I think," she said. "The cross strap on the black ones shortens up your leg a bit."

"Oh, terrific," said her mother, in mock disgust. "Remind me never to wear *those* again."

"No, Mom, they're great with pants!" said Alex. "I'm the one who talked you into buying them, remember?"

Her mother took off her black sandal and donned the other beige one. "Good? I know the party doesn't start until noon, but I need to cut up your father's brownies and pay a pile of bills."

Alex slid off the bed. "Hold still. You have clay in your hair right here."

Her mom smiled. "You can take the girl out of the pottery studio," she said, "but you can't get the pottery clay out of the girl's hair."

Alex smiled. "How do *I* look?" She twirled a little, causing her green sundress to swish around her.

"Gorgeous," said Mrs. Sackett. "I love your dress. It's perfect with your eyes."

"I just hope I'm not too dressed up," said Alex worriedly. "I have no idea what people wear to a block party around here."

The doorbell rang. Moxy began barking

her head off. Alex and her mom exchanged surprised looks.

"Who could that be?" asked her mom. "It's only a little after eleven. I don't even think Tommy's awake yet."

They heard Ava clattering down the stairs to answer it. Then they heard women's voices in the downstairs hallway.

Mrs. Sackett's eyes widened. "Neighborhood ladies!" she whispered. "Thank goodness I'm already dressed!" Alex pushed her toward the door of her room. "Well, *I'm* not ready!" she whispered back. "I still have to straighten my hair and decide on accessories!"

Her mother headed downstairs while Alex flew around her room, plugging in her straightener, flinging open drawers, and rummaging around. Usually she wouldn't dream of messing up her room like this. Everything was always perfectly neat and put away—things were just easier that way. But under the circumstances, she would have to make an exception.

Ten minutes later she found her mother in the front entryway, standing with a group of women, a stricken look on her face.

"You all just met Ava," she was saying. "This is her twin sister, Alex. Alex, this is Mrs. Kelly, Mrs. Barnaby, Mrs. Cahill, and Mrs. Valdeavano."

Alex smiled politely at them.

"I sent Ava to grab your father from the study," said Mrs. Sackett. "Evidently the party has started early, and we are wanted down the block!"

"But first—your mother was just about to give us a tour of the house!" said Mrs. Kelly, smiling broadly at Alex. "We just can't *wait* to have a glimpse into the Sackett family's domestic kingdom. I love what I see already! Laura, I hear you're very artistic!"

"Oh, ha ha," said Mrs. Sackett. "I'm not so sure that translates into being artistic with home decorating. Alex is my consultant in that department. And we've been so busy we haven't had a whole lot of time to get completely settled yet."

"Oh, no, it's lovely. Just lovely," crowed Mrs. Cahill, as the group moved toward the dining room, which was just off the front entrance. The table was still stacked with boxes.

Mrs. Sackett gave Alex a look that said, *Rescue me!* Alex sprang into action.

"New plan!" she said brightly. "I know that Daddy is eager to get to the party early. Why don't we have Daddy and Ava head over with these ladies now? I'll get Tommy out of bed while you go cut the brownies."

"Good idea, Alex," her mother said, smiling at her gratefully.

"Oh, did you bake brownies for the party?" asked Mrs. Kelly. "How nice!"

"Actually, Michael baked them," said Mrs. Sackett brightly. "He's the baker in our house."

Mrs. Cahill raised her eyebrows. "A man of many talents," she said.

Alex bounded off to get her father and Ava. They were in his study, sitting side by side, watching film. Alex's eye rested briefly on Ava's outfit. Casual, of course. But at least she had a skirt on. Even if it was denim. And her V-neck T-shirt was a pretty pale blue and didn't even have a sports team's logo on it. Alex explained the urgency of the situation. Coach seemed to absorb the problem quickly, and he and Ava headed over to corral the ladies out the front door.

"Thanks, sunshine," said her mother, sighing in relief after the group had departed.

Ava followed behind her father and the group of women. It turned out the block party was not technically on their block. It was at the little park where she'd gone to play basketball and had met Jack.

The paved area near the entrance was set up with several grills and a pit barbecue that was being manned by a couple of dads she didn't know. Behind that was the basketball court and play area, and behind that, an open, grassy field.

Little kids were playing on the playground, and a few boys her age were shooting baskets at the basketball hoop. She looked at them wistfully, and then realized she was all dressed up. She glared down at the T-shirt, skirt, and flip-flops she had on. Alex had insisted that she wear nice clothes for this dumb party, but it was not exactly easy to play basketball in a skirt.

Her father was immediately surrounded by about a dozen people. Ava still wasn't used to seeing him in this role. Not so much a celebrity, because they weren't exactly adoring fans. More like . . . a newly elected president, someone people were thrilled to be seen with and to have their picture taken with, but whom most people were still wary about until he was able to prove himself worthy.

There was Tyler Whitley, who was easy to recognize even out of his uniform, as he was tall, broad-shouldered, and extremely handsome. There was PJ Kelly next to Tyler. He said something to one of the ladies, and Ava realized that it was Mrs. Kelly, and that she must be his mom. Did that explain her coolness toward Coach? She'd definitely been the least friendly to him. When Ava had shaken her hand, it had felt like shaking a glove filled with damp sand.

She moved closer. One of the men was asking her dad about his strategy.

"I heard you were installing the midline read option," the man was saying to Coach. "Against a three-three stack, does the quarterback read the four technique, or who becomes the B gap player?"

She listened as her father gently deflected the question, trying to steer the conversation away from football.

"Tyler should be the X receiver," said Mrs. Kelly, and there was ice in her tone. "Then you'd be able to get him one on one against a weaker corner. But I'm not sure Coach is thinking along those lines, are you, Coach? Not part of your style?"

Ava couldn't hear what her father said in response, but she squirmed with uneasiness on his behalf. She could practically hear the drumbeat of anxiety quickening all around her. Why *was* Coach so hard on PJ and Tyler? Wasn't he worried about losing his job?

"Hey!" said a voice behind her.

It was Jack. He held up a squishy green football. "You up for a toss?"

Ava nodded happily and kicked off her flip-flops. So what if she was wearing a skirt. They headed toward the open, grassy field—perfect for tossing the ball around.

She fell into step with Jack. The dry grass felt warm and tickly under her bare feet. "So you live on this block? I remember the first time I met you was right here."

Jack grinned. "Nah, I live about three blocks away," he replied. "But they're not too strict about it—they use the term 'block party' pretty loosely around here." He looked past her. "There's your sister."

Ava looked. Alex was heading toward them across the grass, her hair shiny and straight, her new sundress pressed and perfect. She really did look nice, Ava had to admit. As Alex drew closer, though, Ava read a distinctly disapproving look on her sister's face.

"Al—I mean, Alex—you remember Jack?" Ava said as her sister approached.

Alex nodded coldly at him. "Yes," she said. "Hi."

"Hey, Alex," said Jack.

Alex barely glanced at him. "So should we go get food, Ava?"

Ava looked at Jack to see if he had picked up on her sister's coldness. If he had, he didn't seem to be bothered by it.

"Jack and I are going to play catch," said Ava shortly.

She took the ball from Jack's grasp, backed up a few paces, and tossed it to him. Alex sniffed, turned on her heel, and headed back toward the party.

What is up with Alex? Ava thought. *Why was she so mean to Jack? What right does she have to be so judgmental?* Anyway, it didn't matter—Ava wasn't even interested in him!

Jack interrupted her thoughts. "So a friend of mine asked me to ask you something," he said, staring down awkwardly at his sneakers.

Ava had no idea what was coming. She braced herself.

"He, uh, he wants to know if, uh, if your sister likes anyone right now." Jack finished the end of his sentence in a rush and looked relieved to have gotten it out.

Ava felt a flood of relief. That was all, then. She was used to guys having crushes on her sister. It wasn't the first time she'd been sounded out on her sister's behalf. But who was it? Her heart sank. What if it was that guy Corey? The one who'd said that if their dad didn't win big, he was "out of here"?

"I—ah—I don't really know," she said, and she realized she was being truthful. Alex seemed to like Corey, but they hadn't really talked about it. She and Alex hadn't had a regular heart-to-heart in a long time. She felt hot tears brimming in her eyes, and her vision misted up. She missed her sister.

Just then Jack hurled the football and she leaped up and caught it. She got into a throwing stance. "Go long!" she called to him. Whatever was wrong between her and Alex only seemed to be getting worse, but Ava couldn't think of a better distraction than playing sports.

CHAPTER ELEVEN

After Alex left Ava and Jack, the first person she saw was her mother, surrounded by some of the ladies who had rung their doorbell. Another woman was heading toward Mrs. Sackett from the other side of the barbecue area, where Coach was also surrounded. The woman was Mrs. Kelly, and Alex realized she must be PJ's mom. She felt a pang of foreboding, remembering what Ava had said. Hadn't Mrs. Kelly been going around saying mean things about their dad's coaching style?

Mrs. Kelly was in midsentence as Alex made her way into the circle next to her mother.

"Oh, there you are, honey," said her mom, in the artificially cheerful voice Alex had come to recognize meant her mom was seriously uncomfortable. "Mrs. Kelly was just talking about the team."

"I was just remarking about your dad's unorthodox approach to practices," said Mrs. Kelly. Alex could tell Mrs. Kelly was agitated, but when she spoke, there was a big smile on her face.

Alex looked worriedly at her mom. *Time to change the subject,* she thought.

"Did you know my mom is an amazing ceramist?" she asked the ladies.

"Oh! How quaint!" said Mrs. Kelly.

Mrs. Sackett shot Alex a grateful look, relieved not to have to talk about the football team.

Alex pushed on. "Yes, and we're designing a new website for her to sell her work. She's already fired over a dozen new pieces."

"I don't know how you do it all, Laura!" said Mrs. Cahill.

"Wait a minute, April, aren't you a surgeon?" asked Mrs. Sackett, laughing. "That's not exactly a low-stress job!"

"Oh, but I'm not the coach's wife," said Mrs. Cahill.

Mrs. Sackett opened her mouth to say

something, and then closed it again. She just smiled and nodded.

Alex started to say something too. She wanted to tell them that back in Massachusetts, her mom had had a full-time job as an art teacher, *and* she'd been the head of a dorm at her husband's old school, *and* she'd never missed one of Ava's or Tommy's games, *and*—but a warning look from her mother made her stay quiet. Ava always seemed to know when to stop talking, but sometimes Alex had a hard time figuring that out. She was having an especially difficult time here, in this new place, with that. She missed Ava. Ava had always been there to help her negotiate this kind of thing.

She turned to look at her twin. There she was on the wide lawn, still throwing a ball around with that scoundrel, Jack, and a few other boys. A lump rose in her throat as she watched her sister gracefully stretch out to catch the football and then fling it, effortlessly, to the next kid. It spun in a perfect spiral into his outstretched hands. She and Ava needed to clear the air. Alex would tell her what she knew about Jack.

She excused herself from the circle of ladies, who had moved on from her mother to discussing college football, and headed back toward her sister. And then she stopped short.

There was a girl heading in the same direction. That Girl. The one she'd seen with Jack at the mall and at the pool. The one who was almost definitely his girlfriend.

Alex looked quickly toward Ava. She was running after a long toss and hadn't seen the girl yet. Would she be devastated? Alex quickened her step.

Close up, the girl was undeniably pretty. She was dressed more casually than Alex was (mental note, Alex thought: Summer block parties call for casual chic for middle-school girls). She had on white shorts that made her long, tanned legs look even longer and more tanned, and a sleeveless navy blouse that was tied in a cute bow at the hem. Her hair was piled carelessly on the back of her head in a bun (mental note, Alex thought: Topknots are out—high buns are in). She had a considerable amount of makeup on, but it looked really good on her.

By the time Alex reached them, the boys and Ava had already trotted in to form a circle and were making introductions.

"Lindsey," said Jack, as Alex joined them. "This

is Ava's sister, Alex, the one I told you about. I guess you can tell they're twins," he added, with a sideways smile.

"Hi," said Alex, a trifle cautiously. She wasn't sure what ground they might be standing on, metaphorically speaking. Would Lindsey be mean to her and Ava, because she knew Ava had been hanging out with Jack? Would she act jealous? Triumphant? Was Ava really upset and not showing it? She certainly didn't look upset.

"You guys look so much alike!" Lindsey exclaimed. Her voice was musical, pretty. Alex detected only the slightest hint of a Texas accent.

To Ava, Lindsey said, "I'm so glad you wear your hair short, or I don't think I'd be able to tell you two apart at all! Have you ever been confused with each other?"

"Our mom says when we were little our dad used to make a mark on Alex's hand so he could tell us apart," said Ava, "but he denies that."

Lindsey giggled. "Well, you sure do look alike. Except for the hair, of course."

Alex kept her face impassive, but inside she was unimpressed. Did this girl not realize that she and Ava had been hearing comments their whole lives about how much they looked alike?

"I think your hair is totally adorable," Lindsey continued. "You look a little like Jenna Zachary on *That's So Awesome!*"

"Thanks," said Ava with a small smile. "I cut it because I thought it would be easier for playing sports and stuff. Plus, it's so hot here."

Lindsey squealed with laughter as if Ava had just said the funniest thing in the world. Alex was even more confused. Was Lindsey being nice, or fake-nice? Why was it so hard to tell? And why did Ava feel the need to explain her haircut to this girl, this stranger, this girlfriend of the boy she liked, when she hadn't ever really bothered to explain it to her own twin sister?

Jack and his friends had stepped away and were chatting together, clearly bored of the talk about hairdos.

"I was so excited when I heard you guys were going to be at the party," Lindsey continued. She turned toward Alex. "Jack tells me you like design and fashion! I just love your dress."

Alex wasn't sure, but she thought maybe Lindsay's tone indicated that she felt quite the opposite about her dress. Alex suddenly had the feeling that she'd worn exactly the wrong thing to this party. She decided she had to do some damage control quickly and show stylish Lindsay that she knew a thing or two about fashion.

"Thanks. I like your top," said Alex sincerely. "It's so retro."

Lindsey's smile grew tighter, but Alex didn't notice.

"Was it your mother's?" Alex went on. "Actually, it looks like it's, like, from the fifties! Maybe your grandmother's?"

"No, it wasn't," said Lindsey through gritted teeth.

"Did you get it from a thrift shop?" Alex pressed.

Lindsay's face was now bright red.

"Alex, I don't think it's retro," said Ava, giving her sister a meaningful look.

Alex finally understood Ava's unspoken message. It meant, *Let it go. Move on.* But what had she said? Why would Lindsey be mad at her for asking about her top? Had Alex said the wrong thing? Had she offended her? She *liked* retro. Thrift shops were all the rage in Boston—Alex and Isabel used to go all the time. Were they not cool in Texas?

Lindsey stepped over to where the boys were standing and hooked her arm through Jack's.

"Your mom wants us to go over to have our picture taken," she murmured in his ear.

Is she using that icky familiar tone with him to upset Ava? Alex wondered. But Ava's expression remained neutral.

"It was so great to meet y'all!" she said over her shoulder as she and Jack walked back toward the barbecue area. "I just can't *wait* till school starts and we can see more of one another!"

There was silence between the twins. The noise of the party receded in the background.

Ava put her hands on her hips. "What is up with you?" she demanded. "Why were you so rude just now?"

"What are you even *talking* about?" Alex asked. "I was totally nice! I just told her I liked her top, didn't I?"

"I didn't mean to Lindsey," said Ava impatiently. "I meant to *Jack*. Both times you've been around him, you've barely looked at him or spoken to him. He's really not cool enough for you, is he?"

Alex seethed. "Why should I be nice to a guy who inappropriately flirts with someone when he already has a girlfriend? I find that totally reprehensible."

"I don't know what reprehensible even means, but I never said I liked him," protested Ava. "Who *cares* if he likes Lindsey?" She started to say something else, then seemed to think better of it, then seemed to decide to say it after all. "And you've been so weird about my haircut."

"Weird how?"

"Like, you've taken it as a personal insult that I cut it short. I just did it for sports. You seem to think a haircut is, like, completely intertwined with popularity. But hair just doesn't really matter to me like it seems to matter to you."

Alex reared back, wounded. "I don't *care* about hair. Well, I do, but not that much. I just thought you were trying so hard to look different, to separate yourself from me. I would never drastically change how I look without consulting you first. We've never ever done that before. You don't even seem to like being twins anymore."

Ava's eyes widened. "*What* are you *talking* about? You're the one who's been ignoring me! Remember at the pool that day? You couldn't get away from me fast enough, to join the popular kids. I was stuck playing with a couple of little kids."

"I thought you liked playing with little kids!

And anyway, Corey was there, and you haven't exactly been pleasant to *him*."

"Corey?" Ava rolled her eyes. "He's kind of a jerk, no offense. I haven't liked him ever since the first day of practice, when I heard him trash-talking Coach. I even heard him say there are no second chances in Ashland."

Their voices were climbing. "You are so wrong about him!" Alex shot back. She couldn't think straight. She was dimly aware of her dad's and Tommy's voices not far away from them, and they also sounded like they were arguing.

"Girls!" hissed their mother, who was suddenly standing between them. "We are *leaving*!"

They both knew enough to obey that tone.

As Ava and Alex wound their way through the crowds of people, Alex tried not to cry. She was aware that everyone was staring at them. Great. Not only was her relationship with her sister in shambles, but so was her reputation. Half the town had witnessed the meltdown. By tomorrow, the *whole* town would know.

Forget class president. She'd be lucky if she got a seat at a decent lunch table. At this point, Ava probably wouldn't even sit with her.

CHAPTER TWELVE

Up in her room, Ava lay on her bed, staring at the ceiling. The house, usually full of laughing, talking, singing, and barking when the whole family was home, was eerily quiet. Her parents were talking in murmurs in their bedroom down the hall, and Tommy was in his room, playing moody songs on his keyboard. She assumed Alex was in her own room, too. *Maybe she's color-coding her sock drawer,* Ava thought, and then immediately regretted it.

Moxy had sensed that something was amiss and had followed Ava upstairs. Now the dog lay alongside her, and Ava stroked her black, brown, and white fur softly. Every so often, Moxy rolled her eyes upward to look worriedly at Ava.

The awful block party kept playing over and over in her head, like a video set to loop. She hadn't really meant to say such mean things to Alex. It must have been the long buildup, the stress about their dad, and—

Their dad. What had he and Tommy been fighting about? Was Tommy upset that he was facing a long season of sitting on the bench? Was he upset because Coach was being rough on him? Or did he really, secretly, deep down, not care that much about football? Maybe Coach sensed that at some level and didn't want to admit that his own son wasn't as passionate about the sport as he was.

Tommy seemed to be good at nearly everything he did. He was a natural athlete, a gifted musician, and charming. Girls fell all over themselves when he was in the room, but he didn't really seem to notice. Ava had always had a special relationship with her brother. She suspected that Alex was a little jealous of their bond, but then, didn't Ava deserve it, just a little? How much more did Alex want? Things always seemed to come so easily to Alex—she was pretty, popular with kids and with teachers, and got good grades. Ava was already dreading the start of school next week. Teachers usually decided by day one that she wasn't a top-notch student, that she wasn't paying attention, that she was a daydreamer. The comparisons to her twin sister that teachers made were never in Ava's favor. So she didn't feel guilty if she was her brother's favorite.

There was a knock at her door, and her dad entered without waiting to be invited.

Moxy raised her head anxiously, saw that it was only Coach, not Mrs. Sackett, and put her head back down on her paws.

"Hey, sport," said Coach. He looked around the room and winced a little. Ava did have to admit, the mustard-yellow color was hard to take in. And the room didn't look very cozy. Boxes were stacked throughout the room, clothes were draped across most surfaces, and none of her posters were on the walls. She really ought to start sprucing it up.

Coach moved into the room with his customary athletic grace. For an older guy, he still had the physique of an elite athlete. Back in high school, he'd been the quarterback and the captain of the basketball and baseball teams. He'd been recruited for both football *and* basketball for college. Ava hoped she had inherited even half of his athletic prowess.

He gave Moxy a gentle shove to the side and sat down on Ava's bed. "Fun party, huh?" he said.

"Super fun," Ava deadpanned, stroking Moxy. "And I didn't even get a barbecued spare rib."

Coach laughed, then was quiet. "Have you and that sister of yours had a talk?"

She shook her head and turned onto her back. "No," she said, crossing her arms. She was quiet for a minute. "We've just gotten really . . . different . . . since we moved here. We don't seem to see eye to eye much."

"She's the best friend you've got, and ever will have, and you know that," he said. "And you know her better than anyone. Alex handles change by taking control over it. Then you changed, but she can't control you."

Now Ava was quiet for a minute.

"I didn't change to hurt her." She sighed. "But I see what you mean. I'll talk to her. But Daddy—" She stopped herself. Should she even bring it up?

"You never call me 'Daddy,' Ave—what's up?" He waited, his clear green eyes searching her face, encouraging her to go on. So she did.

"I'm worried about something else. Alex and I both are."

"About me?"

"Yeah . . . about your job."

"Honey, Alex and I already discussed this. I told her there was nothing to worry about. Besides, we haven't even had our first game yet."

"I know, I know, but I keep hearing gossip. Mostly about what PJ's mom is saying. She's going around bad-mouthing you to anyone who will listen. She says you're hard on some of the players, especially PJ. And that you're not using the receivers and the running backs the right way, or something like that. I'm worried that"—she swallowed down a huge lump that had risen in her throat—"I'm worried that if you keep being hard on the stars on the team, your job might be on the line."

Her dad pressed his lips together and smiled. "Ave, I don't think we have to worry about Mrs. Kelly all that much, to be honest. The other coaches warned me about her long before I even got here. She's infamous around these parts. She's complained about her son's coaches since PJ was just out of diapers, it seems."

"She has?" Ava pushed up to a sitting position,

allowing herself to feel a tiny bit of relief.

"Yes, she has. And PJ is a good kid. A nice kid. But he's lazy. He's such a good athlete, he's never really had to work hard. It's the same thing with Tyler. So far, they've both gotten by on raw talent. But they're at the point now where they need to learn to work hard: to learn the plays, to show up for practice on time and ready to perform, and to become positive contributors. Leaders. That's going to be the difference between a talented team making it to state, and actually *winning* state. We all need to go the extra mile." He sat back and looked reflective. "If I have been a little hard on them, it's for their own good."

"And what about Tommy?" asked Ava in a small voice. "Do you think you've been hard on him, too?"

Her dad looked at her and stroked his scruffy chin. He was silent for a moment before he spoke. "Maybe I have been, honey. Maybe I have been."

painting clothes. "Ava Jane," she said firmly. "We need to paint your room whether you like it or not. You may be fine with that hideous mustard color, but I, personally, can't stand it. School starts next week, so now's the time."

"Okay," Ava said. "I do want to put up my posters."

"Come have some breakfast," Mrs. Sackett commanded. "Then the two of you can move Ava's stuff out into the hallway."

It took most of the morning for Ava and Alex to stack Ava's still-packed boxes into the hallway, along with her posters, which were all still carefully rolled up and stored in special poster canisters.

Alex offered to help their mom prime the room. "It will be so satisfying to get rid of that hideous color," she said.

"Should I help too?" asked Ava.

Alex and their mother exchanged a look. "I think we can do it," said Mrs. Sackett.

The last time Ava had tried to help paint, she'd started daydreaming halfway through and had painted half the ceiling bright red before she realized what she was doing.

So Ava went to practice with Coach and Tommy.

CHAPTER THIRTEEN

No one brought up the party the next day in the Sackett household. It seemed everyone would rather forget it and move on.

Neither Alex nor Ava slept well Sunday night. Early Monday morning Ava climbed out of bed and stumbled sleepily down the stairs to watch some dumb TV.

She discovered that Alex was already sprawled out on the couch. The sisters exchanged a wary look. Ava hesitated, trying to decide if she should stay. Then she shrugged and settled into her usual place at the other end of the couch. Moxy jumped up and nestled between them.

An hour later Mrs. Sackett appeared in the doorway, her hair up in a kerchief, wearing her

That night, Ava and Moxy slept on the couch. Alex had been firm about the danger of breathing volatile organic compounds, but Ava couldn't help notice that Alex hadn't invited her to sleep in *her* room.

The next morning their mom announced that Ava's room was still under quarantine. It was going to require two coats of paint to completely cover up the mustard color. "Why don't you girls go somewhere for the morning?" her mom suggested. "I can drive you wherever you want."

Ava looked at Alex. "You want to head to the pool?" she asked her.

"Can't," said Alex shortly. "I have to study."

Ava's brow furrowed. "Study? School hasn't even started yet."

"I have twenty-five more vocab words to learn," said Alex with a patient sigh. "And I'm taking pre-algebra this year; there are some sample problem sets I found at the back of our new textbook that I want to try."

Ava shrugged. "Okay. Maybe I'll take Moxy to the park and play some basketball."

"Good idea," said her mom.

Half an hour later, Ava let the screen door slam shut behind her and Moxy—she was gradually becoming acquainted with the new house, but she kept forgetting that the screen door slammed. They set off on foot for the park. Moxy strained at the leash, thrilled to be on an unplanned outing on top of her morning walk.

Ava's large sports bag bumped against her back with each step—it had been a birthday present from Alex last year, a special backpack that had a net pouch large enough to accommodate a basketball or a soccer ball. This time she had even remembered to pack some water for herself and for Moxy in it.

As they got closer to the basketball court, Moxy suddenly strained on the leash and pulled her along the sidewalk faster. Ava looked up. It was Jack. He was heading toward the park from the other direction, riding his bike.

He slowed to a stop at the entrance and waited for her and Moxy to catch up.

"Hey," he said, grinning.

"Hey yourself," she said back, feeling her ears get hot.

Moxy sniffed his leg and looked at him adoringly, her tail wagging back and forth like crazy.

"Guess Moxy likes you," said Ava.

"All dogs love me," Jack admitted, stooping

down to ruffle Moxy's head. "I can't explain it. I don't have a dog myself, because my mom's allergic. But most dogs I know just seem to decide their lives will be incomplete if they can't spend every moment in my presence."

Ava laughed. Her heartbeat quickened a little too. Not only was he an athlete, but he was funny. It was always so great to discover that someone had a good sense of humor.

"Do you come here a lot?" she asked him, as they headed toward the court.

He hesitated. "Well, I ride by here a lot," he said. "These days."

What does that mean? she wondered. *Was he looking for someone? Was he hoping to see me?* No. That was stupid. He had a girlfriend—that Lindsey person. Although Ava wouldn't have guessed Jack would date someone like Lindsey. She shook her head. She really needed to stop with these dopey thoughts.

"You brought your ball," he said. "Okay if I shoot around with you? There's usually a game going on here—guys from AMS mostly—but I guess it's a little too early in the day."

"Sure," said Ava. "If you're not afraid I'll school you again."

"Oh, I'm very afraid," he said with a grin.

Ava instructed Moxy to sit and stay, and the dog obediently sat at the edge of the court to watch them. A squirrel darted up a tree nearby, and Moxy looked at it longingly but stayed where she was.

"Wow, that's impressive," said Jack, gesturing toward Moxy.

"I know," said Ava. "My sister trained her. She's not the most well-behaved dog on the planet, but Alex insisted on teaching her a few basic rules."

"That does seem to fit with your sister's personality," he said.

Ava wondered if she should follow up his comment and apologize to him for her sister's coldness. But it seemed too . . . personal. She kept silent.

Jack was checking a text on his phone. He bounce-passed the ball to her. "Some guys are showing up here in a little while. Maybe we can get a game going."

"Sure," said Ava. She hit a bank shot and moved to the next spot around the circle. "Is, um, Lindsey a basketball player?"

"Lindz? Ha. No. Strictly girly stuff like cheerleading," he said, passing the ball back to her.

Ava's next shot clanged off the rim and rolled away.

Jack trotted after the ball and then held it. He looked at her steadily. "There's something you should know about me and Lindz," he said.

A few hours later Ava burst through the kitchen door; she couldn't wait to tell Alex her news. She and Jack, and, later, some of Jack's friends, had played several games of full-court basketball, and she had played well. She and Moxy had jogged all the way home, and now Moxy went straight to her water dish. But except for Moxy's loud lapping, the house was surprisingly silent.

Of course, Coach and Tommy would still be at practice. But where were Mom and Alex?

"Hello?" Ava called.

No answer.

Then she saw the note on the kitchen table in Alex's perfect handwriting.

We're upstairs.

Puzzled, she set down her backpack and headed through the kitchen and up the stairs.

"Mom? Al?"

No answer. Another note lay at the top of the stairs. She picked it up.

We're in your room.

Was she in trouble? Had something bad happened in her room? Maybe she'd left a box of tissues on the floor again, like she'd done once back in Massachusetts, where Moxy had spent a delightful morning chewing them up one by one and leaving them all around her bedroom. Her mom had not been happy with her. But that *couldn't* be. Moxy had been with her all morning.

She put her hand on the knob and slowly turned it. "Hello?" she said. Cautiously, she pushed the door open.

"Surprise!" shouted Alex and Mrs. Sackett at the same time.

The first thing she saw was Alex's face; her expression was both hopeful and nervous. Then she saw the same expression on her mother's face. Then she saw the room.

They had painted it, but it was not beige. It was a light, pretty blue. All her sports posters were up on the walls. They'd unpacked all her boxes of books and trophies and arranged everything neatly on the shelves. They'd even rearranged the furniture, so now her bed was in the corner under the window. She could sit on the end of the bed and actually see outside. There were new curtains, a bedspread, and a rug, all complementary blues, greens, and corals. It wasn't overly decorated; it was just homey—and it was perfect.

Ava's mouth fell open.

"Do you like it?" asked Alex breathlessly.

Ava nodded slowly. "It's awesome."

Alex and Mrs. Sackett let out a collective sigh of relief.

"How did you have time to do all this?" asked Ava. "I haven't been gone very long."

"I did the second coat last night," said Mrs. Sackett. "So the paint was already dry. We were able to do the rest this morning. It was all Alex's idea. She came with me to choose the paint, and she made the curtains and the bedspread last week, with Grandma's old sewing machine. I didn't even know she knew how to use it."

Alex shrugged modestly. "I didn't. But you can teach yourself anything on the Internet," she said.

Ava opened her arms, and her mom and Alex stepped into her embrace.

"Thanks, you guys," she said. "Honestly, I didn't think I cared what my room looked like, but now I see how much I do. It feels like home now."

CHAPTER FOURTEEN

Mrs. Sackett headed downstairs to get lunch ready, leaving Alex and Ava alone in the room. They sat on the bed. Alex watched Ava stroke the pretty pattern. She was so happy Ava liked her room! Using the old sewing machine had been tricky at first, but once she'd gotten the hang of it, things went pretty smoothly. And Ava had made it easy for Alex to keep the curtains and bedspread a secret, because she'd been off so much watching Coach's practices.

Moxy nosed open the door and plopped herself down at their feet, heaving a contented sigh.

They both started to say something, and then laughed.

"You first," said Ava.

"No, you first," said Alex.

"I just wanted to say thanks for doing this," said Ava. "I was starting to think you didn't want to hang out together much. Or that you didn't care that much about, well . . ." She trailed off and looked away.

"I thought you felt the same way," said Alex, putting a hand on her sister's knee. "When my room was being painted, I was waiting for you to ask me to sleep in your room, but you didn't. So I thought you didn't want me to."

Ava's eyes widened. "I thought *you* didn't want to!" she said. "I've really missed sharing a room with you, to be honest."

"Thanks for saying that," said Alex. "I've missed sharing with you, too. And also?" She stopped and swallowed.

Ava waited.

"Also?"

"Still here, Al," said Ava gently.

"Also? I just wanted to say that . . . that . . . I really like your hair. I'm sorry I made you feel like I was embarrassed of you. I think you look amazing."

"Thanks, Al," Ava said gratefully. "That means a lot. Especially considering you're more in touch with hair trends than anyone else on the planet."

Both sisters laughed—the same throaty laugh that was uniquely theirs. One more thing they had in common.

Alex heard a car pull up in the driveway. Coach and Tommy were home from practice.

Ava got up and shut the door. She came back to sit closer to Alex, her eyes shining. "I was looking for you because I wanted to tell you something. About Jack."

Alex nodded, waiting. What was Ava going to say? That Jack had asked her out? She braced herself.

"He and Lindsey are not boyfriend and girlfriend," said Ava.

Alex's eyes narrowed suspiciously. That was impossible—she had seen them together all over town!

"They're *cousins*, Al. Cousins."

"Oh!" said Alex, rearing back in surprise. "So . . . they're cousins?"

Ava laughed. "Yes! He told me just now, when we were playing basketball. I think he wanted me to know because, well, maybe because he might like me. I wasn't sure what I thought about him. I'd just started liking Charlie back home, and then we moved, and then I didn't know if I wanted to think about any boys that way, but now, well, now I don't know."

Alex nodded. "That makes me feel so much better. I hated not liking the guy I knew you had a crush on. I was only being rude to him because I was being protective of you."

"Yeah, that's the same reason I haven't been very friendly to Corey," said Ava. "See, a couple of weeks ago, I was sitting near him and his friends in the stadium seats, and he didn't know who I was, and I heard him say that his dad predicted Coach would be fired if the team didn't have a winning season. So I sort of thought that was a mean thing for him to repeat. And I decided I didn't like him. And then I realized you *like* liked him."

Alex put a hand to her forehead, nodding. It all made sense now. She remembered the conversation she'd had with Corey. "He told me about that. He told me what his dad said, but there was more to it. I think you didn't hear the whole thing."

"I didn't?"

"No—he said his dad *did* say that's what people in the town were saying, but that his dad thinks Daddy is an awesome coach and that people need to give him a season to *rebuild*." She made air quotes with her hands.

"Oh," said Ava. "I guess I shouldn't be so quick to judge people. I have a tendency to do that."

"It's just part of your personality," said Alex. "You're better at figuring people out than I am. In fact, maybe you can help me figure out what was up with Lindsey. I get the feeling she doesn't really like me, and I don't know why. I'm perplexed."

"I might know," said Ava thoughtfully.

"Really?"

"Well, yeah. Jack told me something else about Lindsey. He told me that she and *Corey* were really close, and by the end of last year it seemed like they were more than close. Like, they might be going out."

"Okay, go on," Alex said, listening carefully.

"Yeah, but then suddenly something happened and they weren't together anymore. That might have something to do with why she wasn't so nice to you. Maybe she still likes him. And knows he likes you. It's pretty obvious that he does. He gets all red and trips over stuff."

Alex nodded anxiously. Maybe it *was* true, if Ava had noticed. Ava was almost never wrong about stuff like that.

"Jack thinks it might have been something that happened between Corey's parents and Lindsey's parents," Ava continued. "Some kind of business deal. Jack didn't know much about it, but he thinks maybe Lindsey's family might be kind of short on money because the deal fell through."

Alex buried her face in her hands. "Now I understand why she was not pleased with my comment about her outfit being *retro*. She probably thought I was teasing her about wearing hand-me-down clothes or something like that. Ugh. How on earth am I going to fix this?"

"I don't think you should worry about it," said Ava. "I just—"

She stopped. There were loud voices coming from downstairs. It was Coach and Tommy. They were having a *shouting* argument.

Ava and Alex looked at each other and then they hurried out of the room to see what was going on.

They stopped at the bottom of the stairs. The shouting match was happening in the kitchen.

"Dad!" they heard Tommy say. "I don't care that much!"

"You have to care!" Coach shouted back. "I can't show favoritism toward you—don't you understand that?"

"I do!" said Tommy.

"That means you have to work four times harder than the next guy, and I'm just not seeing that, son!" said their dad.

Then they heard their mom. "Michael. Tommy. *Both* of you. Please."

There was a low murmuring the girls couldn't hear. Then Tommy burst out of the kitchen. He stopped abruptly when he saw the girls standing side by side at the bottom of the stairs. Without a word, he pushed past them and ran up to his room.

A second later their parents emerged from the kitchen, their faces grim.

"Girls. Go play," said their mom distractedly. She and their dad went into the office and closed the door.

Ava raised her eyebrows at Alex. They knew it was wrong to listen in on private conversations, of course. But they silently agreed to walk very, very slowly upstairs. If they overheard something, well then, they did. It was rare that their parents argued. This sounded like a family issue, and they needed to be included.

". . . under so much stress. Maybe this was a mistake," they heard Coach say.

"It's Tommy's decision, Michael," Mrs. Sackett said.

"Maybe I've ruined his chances, Laura. He was the star last year. I think that's why I'm pushing him so much."

"Well, maybe you should *stop*—" Their mother must have realized her voice was getting shrill, because it suddenly dropped to a murmur. "*Murmur murmur murmur* do something fun, to bond with the team," they heard their mother say.

"Laura, I can't do something like that," said their father, the frustration rising in his voice. "The team wouldn't take me seriously, and I can't afford—"

"Shhhh!"

"*Murmur murmur murmur.*"

"Pssssst," whispered Alex, who was standing one step above Ava. "I think I just had an idea. A *stupendous* idea. Come on. Let's go find Tommy. We'll definitely need him for this."

CHAPTER FIFTEEN

The following afternoon, another sweltering day, the team's afternoon practice ran until four. Alex and Ava had convinced first Tommy, and then their mom, that their plan would work.

"This is either a very good idea or a really, really terrible one," said their mom anxiously, as she parked the car behind the stadium.

"It's a good one," said Ava.

"A stupendous one," added Alex.

Alex and Ava jumped out of the SUV and opened the back hatch. They pulled out two large bins and staggered from the parking lot toward the playing field carrying them. Their mom followed a few steps behind.

At the edge of the field, Ava set down her bin

with a grunt. Alex did the same. Both girls sat down on top of their bins and surveyed the scene.

The team was lined up for end-of-practice sprinting. It was still fearsomely hot, despite being after four, and Alex could see a lot of red faces and weary expressions. She spotted Coach Byron's kids and pointed them out to Ava.

"Hey!" Ava called to them, waving them over.

They dropped their coloring books and raced over to her, each giving her a big hug.

"We need your help," said Ava in a conspiratorial tone.

"Ava, are you sure you want them involved?" asked their mom. "It's bad enough that you girls are implicated in this. I don't want *them* to get in trouble too."

But it was too late. Jamila and Shane were jumping up and down excitedly without even knowing what the plan was.

"Tommy's going to give us the signal," said Alex, without taking her eyes off the players in the field. "He's going to take off his helmet, put it back on, and take it off again. That's our cue."

Their mother let out a low, anguished moan in response.

At last Coach blew the whistle, looking stern,

and the team converged on him and the assistants. The boys all took a knee and removed their helmets. Coach began talking to them.

Alex couldn't hear what he was saying. Probably the usual end-of-practice talk, but his expression was stern and his posture was ramrod straight, which Alex knew meant he was mad. His lecture seemed to go on and on. She wondered if he had even noticed they were there.

At long last, Coach ended his talk. Alex's muscles tensed. She stared at Tommy.

But no, now the other coaches had to have their say. More time passed. Alex felt drops of perspiration trickle down her neck. She pulled a hair tie off her wrist and expertly twisted her long hair—curly today—into a bun at the back of her head. Ava, on the other hand, had run her hands through her hair, making it spike straight up. Alex reached over and pulled a piece, giggling. Ava grinned back and shrugged.

At last, the boys stood up and formed a tight group. Tommy stayed toward the outer edge and glanced their way meaningfully. The team let out a loud series of rousing "Go! Go! Go!" shouts.

Tommy put his helmet back on. Then he took it off.

That was their cue.

Ava and Alex flung the lids off their bins.

The team's tight grouping moved apart. Guys turned toward the locker room. Coach stood near the center of the group, glancing down at his clipboard.

Ava pulled out two water balloons and handed a pink one to Jamila and a green one to Shane, along with a whispered instruction to wait for the signal. Then she handed a blue one to Alex and selected a red one for herself. Mrs. Sackett stood to the side, wringing her hands with anxiety.

They'd agreed ahead of time that Ava would throw first. She had the better arm by far.

She took a few steps into the field. Planted her right foot. Stepped with her left. Cocked her right arm and let the balloon fly.

Ava was, after all, her father's daughter. And her brother's sister. Even Alex could see she had inherited the Sackett Arm. Her aim was perfect.

SPLAT!

The balloon exploded against Coach's shoulder and burst, drenching the front of his shirt and a good portion of the papers on his clipboard.

He let out a startled yell and jumped backward as though he had been shot.

Everyone on the field froze. Alex felt as though all the blood in her veins had suddenly dropped fifty degrees. She heard a pounding in her ears.

A flash of green and then pink flew past her. *SPLAT!*

Jamila's balloon hit Coach Byron squarely in the stomach. Shane's went wide, grazed another of the coaches, and burst when it hit the turf. Oblivious to the tension all around them, the kids erupted into peals of laughter.

Their laughter was infectious. The boys, frozen with shock and awe, began to smile, then chuckle. Jamila and Shane scooped up more balloons.

Alex's eyes were fixed on Coach's face. It was dark with anger. *Uh-oh.* They were in big trouble.

Then Tommy trotted over and grabbed Ava's bin and hauled it toward some of the players on the field. Several of them reached in and grabbed balloons, and soon there was an all-out water balloon battle. Laughter, howls, running, more laughing.

Alex stole another glance at her father. The corners of his mouth were tugging upward into a tiny smile. In one swift movement, he dipped into the bucket, hauled out a balloon, and launched it at Coach Byron.

Alex turned. Even their mother had joined the fray!

She felt Ava tugging her by the hem of her shirt. She turned. Ava was smiling. Her eyes were bright with relief and triumph. For the first time in a long time, Alex felt like she and her sister were feeling the exact same thing.

"It worked, Al!" Ava whispered. "They're having fun! And it was your idea!"

Alex linked arms with her sister. "Yep, but you made it happen."

"And look at Coach," Ava continued. "He just pelted Tommy with a balloon. He doesn't look mad at us. Nice going, Al. It really was a great—I mean a *stipendous* idea."

"*Stu*pendous," corrected Alex automatically.

"Yeah. That."

"Ave, let's not fight any more, okay?"

"Okay. We make a much better team when we don't fight," agreed Ava. "Next week when school starts? We'll be—"

"Unstoppable."

"Unstoppable."

They laughed. They'd both said the word at the same time.

It was a twin thing.

Ready for more
ALEX AND AVA?
Here's a sneak peek at the next book
in the **It Takes Two** series:

Two Cool For School

"Perfect."

Alex Sackett stared down at the pale-yellow wrap dress she'd laid out on her bed and nodded with satisfaction. Combined with her brand-new, first-ever pair of cowboy boots, it would be just the right first-day-of-school outfit. She even had a matching yellow headband to wear with it. *Whew!* Alex thought. *Talk about a down-to-the-wire decision. School starts tomorrow!*

She frowned at the heap of discarded clothes on the floor. She'd had to try on half her wardrobe before arriving at the perfect combo, so it was going to take a while to get her room back in shape. And she still had new vocabulary cards to memorize—she tried to memorize five each day.

Alex guessed that her twin sister, Ava, was not laying out her school outfit or memorizing vocab words. Ava wasn't someone you'd describe as a slave to fashion. Just last week she'd appeared at breakfast wearing one of their brother Tommy's T-shirts, inside out. Nor was Ava the plan-ahead type. Alex hoped that maybe this year she'd be able to convince Ava to try getting her stuff ready the night before, so their mornings would be less rushed. Alex loved her twin sister, but she could be pretty disorganized.

The smell of cookies wafted up the stairs, and Alex heard the oven door slam.

"Al! Tommy! Cookies!" yelled Ava from the kitchen.

With one backward glance at the outfit she'd chosen—maybe she should go with the green dress instead?—Alex headed downstairs.

"Second batch will be out in just a couple more minutes," said their dad, Mike Sackett—or Coach, as Ava and Tommy called him. He had tied on one of Mrs. Sackett's ruffled aprons, which made Alex giggle. It was a funny accessory on such a big, athletic-looking guy, complemented by the flowery oven mitts he wore to pull cookies out of the oven. Coach loved to bake, and it was a Sackett family tradition to have milk and cookies the night before the first day of school.

"Got that outfit all set, Al?" asked Ava with a mischievous grin as Alex poured herself a glass of milk. Ava was sitting at the kitchen table, with their school schedules side by side in front of her. They had gone to Ashland Middle School earlier that day to pick them up and take a tour.

"Ave, don't tease your sister," said Coach as he transferred cookies to a cooling rack. Moxy, the Sacketts' energetic Australian shepherd, sat beneath him, waiting hopefully for a cookie to fall to the floor. "It's natural to be a little nervous for your first day at a new school. New town. New state. It's a big change."

"I'm not nervous so much as apprehensive," said Alex, who liked to work her vocab words into sentences as often as possible. She sat down next to her sister to look at their schedules.

"We don't have a single class together," said Ava with a frown. "Not even homeroom."

"We have the same lunch period," Alex noticed.

"You have Mr. Kenerson, the middle school football coach, for homeroom," Ava said, pointing to the name at the top of Alex's schedule.

"Oh, great," she said, blowing back a stray curly tendril that had escaped her ponytail. "You're the one who knows football, but I get the coach. He'll probably expect me to know every play in Daddy's playbook."

"Maybe it'll inspire you to learn a little about the game," said Ava. Their dad set a platter of cookies in front of them, and she helped herself to one of the biggest ones, which was still gooey in the center. "I mean, we have just moved to a football-crazy part of Texas, and our dad is the head coach at the high school."

"Studying up on the rules is definitely on my to-do list," said Alex. "Look, you have Ms. Kerry for homeroom. She's my math teacher."

"Awesome, she'll expect me to be as brilliant as my twin sister," said Ava drily.

Just then their mother burst into the kitchen with the phone in her hand. Her eyes were shining. "Guess what? I just got my first big—and I mean big—order!"

"Aw, honey, that's terrific!" said Coach. He tugged off his oven mitts and gave her a hug.

"What's the order for, Mom?" asked Alex. Their mother was a potter, and Alex had recently helped her create a new website to sell her pieces.

"Remember Katie McCabe, Daddy's colleague back at the old school in Massachusetts? She's registering with me for her wedding!" said Mrs. Sackett. "I'll be making plates, bowls, coffee cups, serving platters—the works!"

"I knew your business would take off fast," said Alex. "You're so talented, Mom."

"Of course she's talented," said their older brother, Tommy, walking into the kitchen with his easy athletic gait. "Where do you think I get all my talents from?" He grinned and put an arm around his mother's shoulders. Alex was still not used to seeing her sixteen-year-old brother looming over their mom. He'd probably grown six inches in the past six months. He was looking more and more like their dad every day—he wasn't as bulky as Coach yet, but he was getting there.

"It's going to be a busy next few weeks, Michael," said Mrs. Sackett, helping herself to a cookie. "I was talking with April Cahill earlier today, and she casually mentioned that as the coach's wife, I'm more or less expected to plan a barbecue for the team for Homecoming weekend. And evidently your predecessor's wife gave each player a towel with his initials embroidered on it!" She shook her head and chuckled in disbelief.

Alex studied her dad's face. He laughed along with her mom, but it was an uneasy laugh.

Belle Payton isn't a twin herself, but she does have twin brothers! She spent much of her childhood in the bleachers reading–er, cheering them on–at their football games. Though she left the South long ago to become a children's book editor in New York City, Belle still drinks approximately a gallon of sweet tea a week and loves treating her friends to her famous homemade mac-and-cheese. Belle is the author of many books for children and tweens, and is currently having a blast writing two sides to each It Takes Two story.